# A CIRCLE OF SILVER

# A CIRCLE OF SILVER

## MAXINE TROTTIER

**Fitzhenry & Whiteside**

OTHER BOOKS IN THE CIRCLE OF SILVER CHRONICLES:
*By The Standing Stone*
*Under a Shooting Star*

Published in Canada in 1999 by Stoddart Kids
Published in the United States in 2000 by Stoddart Kids

Published by Fitzhenry & Whiteside Ltd.
195 Allstate Parkway,
Markham, ON L3R 4T8


4 5 6 7 8 9

**Canadian Cataloguing in Publication Data**
Trottier, Maxine
A circle of silver
(The circle of silver chronicles)
ISBN 0-7737-6055-5
I. Title.

PS8589.R685C57   1999   C813'.54   C99-930792-4
PZ7.T7532Ci   1999

Cover illustration: Al Van Mil
Cover and text design: Tannice Goddard

 Canada Council   Conseil des Arts
for the Arts   du Canada

 ONTARIO ARTS COUNCIL
CONSEIL DES ARTS DE L'ONTARIO

We acknowledge for their financial support of our publishing program the Canada Council, the Ontario Arts Council, and the Government of Canada through the Book Publishing Industry Development Program (BPIDP).


Printed in Canada

*For Bill and the
history we live together.*

*Long ago there were two girls. An ocean of saltwater separated them; the different worlds in which they were born and lived were even wider than that. They did not ever meet. Yet in the end, each one felt in her heart that she had somehow known the other. Something as small as the seed of an apple planted in friendship, as quiet as a thought sent out to another, as simple and perfect as the curve of a silver ring, formed a bond between them. Someday a young English boy would bring them together. But in 1760 on a dark, windy night, neither Lady Jane MacNeil nor Marie Magdelaine Roy knew the other existed.*

# CHAPTER
# ONE

A figure stood at the open window, backlit by flickering candlelight. Young John MacNeil rested his palms against the stone ledge and leaned out into the soft English night. A spring breeze ruffled his hair, set the sleeves of his shirt flapping, and caused the slightly open door of the room to shift. John could not see the ocean that lay beyond Brierly's sloping lawns, but he could hear the low wash of waves against its cliffs. The sea called to him somehow; in a few days he must answer that call.

John stepped back and closed the casement windows. The sheer draperies that had fluttered about like the pale wings of birds settled back into place. He walked around his room, picking up things and putting them back again, then stopped to absently retie his long dark hair with a narrow ribbon. Jars of paints, pots of delicate brushes for his paintings, tiny dried-up starfish, and the shells of long-gone snails cluttered the shelves and tables. He looked up suddenly at the small scratching of claws on the polished wood of the hallway. There was Winston, his twin sister Jane's odd little terrier, peeking in from around the door.

"Come in, Winston," John called cheerfully. "Have you heard the news?" John had spent the hours since morning trying to set a single fact clearly in his mind. It still did not seem to be real, he thought. In a few days he would leave this room behind and sail to Canada with his father, Captain Lord MacNeil. The prospect both thrilled and terrified him. "I hardly think I am the best choice for it," he confided to the little dog.

John was the younger son of Lord MacNeil. He did not care much to ride or hunt like his older brother, David. John fell from horses and out through carriage doors that were not tightly latched. He did not fear to try anything, but failed at it all. Scratched and bruised and bloody, he would limp in at the end of an outing. The damp, musty quiet of the library seemed to suit him more. He spent many hours there each day, bent over the drawings and paintings that took so much of his time. Often his sister, Jane, was with him.

John dropped down onto his bed, carefully avoiding the charcoal sticks and papers that lay on the coverlet. A bottle of ink and a pot of swan's quills stood on the table nearby. He had been drawing, as was his habit each night. Not even the half-packed trunks and the threat of Canada had changed that ritual.

"How can all this have happened in less than a day?" John asked Winston, remembering the morning. But Winston had no answers. He only snorted, shook himself, and then pattered out down the hall on another mission. John thought about his father. Lord MacNeil

had been home for some months. He had returned to
England to report to the Crown with dispatches from
the British military in Canada. Prince George, the eldest
grandson of the King, was most keen to know about
Canada. Lord MacNeil's decision concerning John's
future had not been lightly made. He had carefully
considered the matter all during the long sea voyage that
brought him back to his family. The announcement of
his plans that morning had been received with horror
by his wife, Lady Emma. John himself had been quite
stunned.

"Canada?" he said slowly to his father. "I had not
thought to ever see it." John had always known only
Brierly with its soft-spoken servants and quiet halls.
Canada was said to be a savage place.

"Well, see it you shall," answered his father. "Now off
with you. We leave in two days and you must sort out the
things you will take along." And in the brisk way Lord
MacNeil dealt with all his offspring, John was dismissed
to wander back to his room, shocked and strangely
excited at the same time. He was not surprised to see
Jane standing just outside the door of the morning room.

"Did you hear?" John asked her softly. Jane nodded,
wide-eyed, and set her finger across her lips; she must
know more. John shook his head at this and left her to
her spying.

"In your room tonight," Jane mouthed before he
turned to the staircase. They would meet later as they
often did when the house slept. It was then that
they would talk about what had happened that day.

"My dear," James MacNeil said to his wife, Lady
Emma, from behind the closed door, "a trip to Canada
will make a man of John. He is too soft, you know." They
were in the morning room, lingering over their breakfast.

In fact, it was Lady Emma who was lingering. She
meant to discuss this matter further with her husband
and perhaps sway his thinking. But she sensed that
James's mind would not change regarding the course
John's life would take. MacNeil shifted restlessly in his
chair now and again. He drew his dark brows together in
a slight frown. He was anxious for breakfast to be over so
he could get to the stables, but Emma was delaying. She
was a fine woman, he felt great love for her, but she had
no sense when it came to certain issues. A servant came
into the room.

"Shall I clear, mum?" she whispered.

"Not just yet." Lady Emma picked up her coffee cup
and pretended to sip at it. She had no power over this
man who came and went in and out of her life like some
cyclone. To make him wait endlessly, a victim of his perfect manners, was her small revenge this morning. The
servant girl backed out of the room and disappeared.

"He is not soft at all, James," she insisted. "He is
thirteen years old. There is war in Canada and he is only
a child." She would have none of her children part
from her any sooner than they must. David would never
leave. The eldest son, two years older than his brother
and sister, he would inherit the title and the estate to
become Viscount MacNeil of Brierly. Jane, of course,
would marry. Who could say where marriage and duty

would take her? She was not a pretty child; marriage would be more of a political undertaking than a romantic one, Lady Emma feared. For certain, it would be far from here, perhaps to the Court of King George itself. Her head ached with the thought of it all. She rested her hand lightly upon her belly. And now there was a fourth child coming. Lady Emma sighed. Canada indeed!

"There is no life for him here, my dear, you know that yourself," said MacNeil, leaning toward his wife. "Would you see him in London, gambling away what little money David will give him as an allowance when he comes into his own? If you consider it carefully, you shall see that my plan is the best for John." Lord MacNeil thumped the table heartily and stood up.

"You will kill him." There was a surprising note of anger in his wife's voice. She seldom opposed him in anything.

"He will likely do that himself, given the opportunity," her husband remarked dryly. He pulled his waistcoat straight and picked up his gloves. "John will fall backward out of a chair or a great pile of moldy books will drop off the library shelves and brain him. As for the war, it is only a matter of time until Canada will be British soil.

"Remember, King George is elderly and not well and in time his grandson will come to the throne. You should be pleased that John will have a part in his interests. Besides, my dear, there is the new baby to think of. You will have your hands and arms full in a few months."

The French and English had been at war forever,

it seemed to Lady Emma. This particular horror had broken out some years ago across the ocean in Canada. It was a wild place, she heard, filled with unmanageable people and cursed with extreme weather. But there was the fur trade and that was important to the British Crown. It was equally important to France. Both countries would have the land no matter what the cost. And James thinks to take my son into that! raged Lady Emma.

"He cannot be a soldier, James. It is ridiculous!" she argued. She stood clutching her napkin with white knuckles.

"I agree," answered her husband coolly, and Emma widened her eyes in surprise. "He does not have the makings of a soldier."

"Then what in the world will you have him do?" Her hopes rose.

"He draws better than anyone I know," MacNeil explained as he pulled on his gloves and smoothed the thin cloth over his fingers. "The Crown wants maps and sketches. John shall draw them."

"Not a soldier then. You promise," said Lady Emma sternly.

"Never fear, he will not become a soldier. Besides, he cannot shoot. It would be a waste of powder and he might end up shooting off his own foot. Or mine!"

"You are cruel, Papa," said a young voice crossly. "John is far too clever to do something like that." Jane had drifted into the room unnoticed. She loved her brother very much and did not like to see him criticized. She defended John whenever a word was spoken against him by anyone.

Lord MacNeil looked across at his daughter. She was elfin, all dusty freckles, dusty-colored hair. Serious, calm pale-gray eyes, wide in her narrow face. Except for those eyes, she and John, although twins, did not look alike at all. John's dark locks bent with her ashy curls over some nonsense in the library always slightly surprised Lord MacNeil.

"Do not be insolent, Jane, no one likes an insolent girl," said her mother. Lady Emma sat again and stirred her coffee furiously. John would leave with her husband; the war was lost but a small battle had been won. He would not fight, at least.

"Fine advice, my dear," said Lord MacNeil. He patted Jane on the head and, nodding affectionately to his wife, turned to leave the morning room. "You will see it is for the best. It will be a fine adventure for the boy. And he will love it because it will make a man of him."

Lord MacNeil walked down the hall, his leather boots echoing solidly, thinking about his odd family. He himself was very steady, a military man, and he was not altogether comfortable in this house. He had in Emma a wife who sometimes seemed a stranger and in his children three offspring who could not have been more different from each other if it had been planned. David was the only one who was the least bit like himself, he believed, hard and manly, with just the right whiff of horse and salt air about him. Shaking his head, Lord MacNeil put it all from his mind and turned his thoughts to his morning ride.

Jane stood at the French doors and watched her father descend the front steps two at a time. Great changes took place whenever her father came home from sea, and it seemed this time was to be no different. The entire household sighed in relief when Lord MacNeil sailed or rode off again to conquer some new country for the King. What a sad sigh it was going to be when John left with his father.

"John will travel with Papa this time," stated Jane, watching Lord MacNeil near the stables.

"Yes, he will, and not a thing I say will change it. Perhaps your father is right. Perhaps it will be an adventure." Once, before her marriage, Lady Emma had wanted to have an adventure. Dancing with young Lord MacNeil at Court, held tightly in his clasp, she felt that he would be her adventure. She had been spirited and hopeful then, a lovely woman whose simple beauty had been the toast of London that season. Now her head ached.

"John has exciting things to do here. He does not need to leave Brierly to have adventures," argued Jane, turning away from the French doors to her mother.

"Wandering the woods, drawing, and painting are not considered to be exciting, my dear," laughed Lady Emma with little humor.

"I think it is all greatly exciting," said Jane stubbornly.

"One day you will see that men consider adventure to be quite another sort of thing. It must be something that nearly kills them."

◇ ◇

John and Jane did not see their parents again until dinner that evening. There was a guest. Lord Elgie was at Brierly, and Jane and John were allowed to dress and come down for the meal. Lady Emma believed this to be a rare treat for them. Jane did not care one way or the other. She did not actually like Lord Elgie. He had a very large stomach and ate far too much. She did like to watch him eat, though. He shoveled in the food and made all sorts of interesting noises as he chewed. Perhaps everyone at Court ate in such a manner. If so, she might try it herself when she went there some day.

"Young John will sail with me from Plymouth in a week, Lord Elgie," announced Lord MacNeil suddenly at dinner. John shifted about in his chair, uncomfortable at the sudden attention. Jane stared silently at her father. David's eyes widened in surprise to hear this interesting piece of news, as Lady Emma heaved a small sigh to think of John's departure.

"What a grand idea, James!" roared Lord Elgie, with his mouth full. Little bits of rare roast beef sprayed across the table. Jane watched in fascination.

After the meal, Jane was sent upstairs; John slipped away a short while later. David remained in the drawing room with his parents and their guest. There would be music, Jane knew. John's tutor, Mr. Walsh, was very accomplished on the harpsichord.

Later that night Jane lay awake in the quiet darkness. Everyone still referred to her bedroom as the old nursery, although there was nothing about the modestly decorated room to suggest babies or even that a young girl inhabited it. She stared up at the bed's canopy. It was a large bed and her slight build made her look like some strange bird in an oversized nest. Her hair, tightly braided for the night, stood in wisps around her head. It would not be held in. Her pale eyes blazed in the darkness and she scowled.

"It is not fair," she whispered fiercely to her terrier, Winston, who had come in from his wanderings to nestle next to her. "David goes to London and rides in the hunt because he is the oldest. John will go to sea because he is the younger son. It does not matter that John and I are twins. I am the girl and so I remain at home. Why must I be the only one left behind?"

The little dog just yawned. Jane stroked the small animal's silky ears and combed its long hair with her fingers. She breathed very softly through her nose. There was a wind blowing that now and then made the old windows give a small rattle in the casements. It was not much of a rattle, though, and Mary, her dear old nurse, slept on, snoring peacefully in her bed in the alcove, her knitting held loosely in her hand. Jane loved Mary almost as much as she loved John and Winston. She was not quite certain about her parents, those distant figures who ruled their lives.

A sudden gust of wind roared through the trees outside the windows. Jane listened to the wild sound. She was not the least bit afraid of the wind. "Why should I be afraid?" she said. "There is nothing that can hurt me. There are no dangerous animals here or wild people." Jane kept this to herself. Late at night when the wind blew hard, Mary could be coaxed to tell stories. Her nurse seemed to believe that children were timid things filled with fear, and they often must be comforted.

So, when storms came, Jane always made a point of seeming terrified. Her face would grow a trifle pale, her large eyes would bulge out a bit more. Then Mary might tell the stories of ships and the sea. Jane felt that she knew the sea even though she had never sailed on it. You could not trust its deep, dangerous waters; her old nurse had told her so. She had lost two husbands to the sea in dreadful storms. "Swallowed whole under the waves, they were, both of them. I would never wed another sailor and I pray you never do." It did make Jane shiver to think of the sea and Mary's lost husbands.

Now late at night in her bed, Jane thought of the ship that would carry John away from her. She felt a small nagging inside herself. It was like an ache and a tiny shiver all in one. She recognized the feeling, or at least she thought she did.

"I think I am afraid," she said aloud, staring into the darkness. The thought of losing her brother suddenly seemed dreadful. She gently pushed back the coverlet and eased herself out of bed. Winston jumped down after her. The polished wood felt cool under her bare feet. She knew from long practice just where to step on the wide, oak boards so they would not creak and wake Mary. The one with the round knot that looked like an old man's face was safe; the paler board next to it was not.

Mary always slept with an old tabby cat. The cat opened its yellow eyes and hissed silently at the terrier as

it and Jane crept past. It blinked once, then closing its
eyes, began purring. Jane turned the latch just so. There
was a way to do it so that only a faint *snick* was heard. She
had developed a great talent for appearing suddenly in
rooms, usually during a conversation the speakers would
have preferred to keep private. She was not a bad child
or even one that had been ill brought up. She was simply
curious and sometimes bored. The only girl in the
house, she knew she had a special place. Little had ever
been expected of her other than to appear clean and
lady-like. It was not a position that would last long,
particularly once marriage loomed in the distance.

Down the dim hall she walked. Brierly was a large
house — not as big as some, but still needing a consider-
able staff. It nestled on the southern coast of England,
two days' travel from the seaport of Plymouth. You could
hear the sea from every room at the back end of the
house. The huge oaks and beeches muffled the sound
of the waves that broke against the cliffs, but on a stormy
night the wind carried up their roar.

John's room was at the end of the hallway. She had to
pass David's quarters, but she knew he would not hear
her. He was a sound sleeper. Jane stole past the staircase,
her long nightdress just brushing the tops of her feet.
The moon shone down through the high windows onto
the runner. Milky light turned Winston's gray-and-tan
coat to silver. It lit Jane's small face and drifting hair.
Then they were in the darkness again. She stopped in
front of John's door.

"I wonder if I think very hard, will he know I am

here?" She put her face close to the door. Her nose nearly touched the wood and her eyes opened wide as she thought of John as hard as she could for nearly a minute. Nothing happened. She opened the door carefully and there was a soft sound as the latch gave way.

John was sitting up in bed, awake as Jane knew he would be. He was not yet dressed for sleep and still wore his breeches and full-sleeved shirt. Jane ran across the carpet with Winston behind her and leaped onto the covers. John leaned over, picked Winston up, and set him on the bed. He brushed his own dark hair from his forehead. With its smooth cheeks and stubborn chin, his face was boyish and open. A smile lit his gray eyes.

"Could you feel me out there?" Jane asked her brother as she peeked at his sketches. John studied his sister's face.

"No." He had known she would come to see his work and give him news, but not exactly when. His sister did like to surprise him.

Jane wanted more than anything else to be like John, but she could not draw or paint. Her pictures of people looked like creatures from another world, all thin legs and round bodies. She could only draw them from the front, not like John who could, with a few swiftly sketched lines and a bit of shading, make his figures come alive. John often gave her drawings and Jane hung them in her room.

"You could not feel me reaching out for your mind?" asked Jane.

"No."

"Well, I was," she said. "I was reaching out with my mind, commanding you to open the door."

"You know I leave it unlocked for you," John answered, smiling. Sometimes he would wake to find his sister's face almost touching his, her breath warm on his skin. Jane seemed to be odd with her staring, but she could not see well and would peer at people very intently to fix their faces in her mind. It bothered most people, her wide, serious gaze, the whites of the eyes showing slightly.

"She looks a bit strange," David had once observed to John, elbowing him smartly to drive home the point. John had not bothered to answer. He did not have Jane's flair for theatrics, but he did admire her talent. He knew his sister was very different from most people. John wondered what would happen to her in time.

He sometimes wondered the same thing about himself. In truth, he tried to be careful as he picked his way slowly through the meadow or the woods, searching for things to save or draw. But he was often lost in thought, staring at the lovely design of a patch of moss or the small creatures in a tidal pool beneath the cliff where they sometimes picnicked. It was then that he might slip or fall over his own feet.

"Watch where you are going," David would laugh. He, naturally, never fell.

"I *was* watching," John might say, brushing seaweed or leaves from his clothing. He did not bother to explain to his brother just what he had been watching, though. Those secret things and what he felt about drawing them, he shared with Jane alone.

"You will leave with Papa," Jane said flatly. She did not believe in avoiding issues; she always got straight to the point.

"Yes, I shall," answered her brother. "Father has made his decision and I can do nothing else."

"Ah, yes," Jane observed. "It is as David always says. Parents are to be obeyed."

John smiled at a memory of David scolding her years ago after she had complained about having less freedom than her brothers. Jane had kicked him very hard in the shin and run off. Given what had happened this morning, however, John thought David might be correct after all.

"But it will not be forever, Jane. I will come home again, you know."

Jane faced her brother, unable to keep her secret any longer. "I heard him say that you will draw maps and pictures of Canada while you are there," she said, giving up her news.

"I see," said John thoughtfully, as his interest was caught. He was, in fact, now somewhat eager about his father's plan. He wondered about the land to which he would travel. He had heard so much about the people and the animals that inhabited that place. It meant an entirely new world for him to draw. He would miss Jane, though. She was one of the only people with whom he could talk. No one could talk to David and one did not really talk to Mama. It occurred to him that he did not know what he would ever talk about with his father.

"When you are away I will come in here every night and sit on your bed. I will send out my thoughts to you," said Jane, stretching out on the coverlet. Jane had always preferred his room to her own. Sitting there each evening would be a comfort once he was gone.

"You must write to me, Jane," John said affectionately. "Letters take a very long while to go back and forth across the ocean, so you will have to tell me a great deal each time."

"I shall," said Jane, "and you will write to me also. You must send many drawings. I want to know exactly how it all looks. It is unfair that you are to have an adventure and I am to stay here. Maybe I should hide on the ship and go with you."

John felt a twinge of discomfort. That was exactly the sort of thing that Jane might do.

"You cannot do that. Promise me you will not even try." Jane was silent for a moment, just to see John squirm a bit and then she said, "Yes, I promise." The idea did have its appeal, though. Perhaps she would marry a pirate.

"You will have Mr. Walsh all to yourself now," John suggested brightly. "Think of that."

Jane did like Mr. Walsh. She had refused a governess, taking her lessons with John and his tutor instead. "Perhaps I shall marry Mr. Walsh while you are away." Jane always enjoyed trying out her new ideas on John first. Her brother picked up a paper and charcoal.

"That is silly," said John absently as he finished a drawing. "Besides, Mama will need your help with the new baby." Lady Emma had no idea that her son knew of her pregnancy. Such things were never discussed in front of children. But Mary's sharp old eyes had seen weeks ago. She had told Jane, who, of course, had shared the wonderful secret with John. In the fall Jane would have a new bedroom in the west wing of the house, overlooking the garden. Mary would stay in the nursery with the baby. John had considered the idea of relocating as well, but now there was no point in doing that.

"Well, I shall not marry until I find someone exactly like me," said Jane, ignoring her brother. John tried to think of such a person, but even he had not that much imagination.

"Take this," Jane said suddenly, and she pulled a ring from her finger. "It is my special ring, you know." The blacksmith, Mr. Plum, had shaped it for her from the handle of an ancient silver spoon she had found while digging in the garden. She liked to imagine that the spoon had belonged to old King Henry. Perhaps the King had eaten his peas with it. "Well, maybe the King did eat his peas with it an' maybe he didn't," said Mr. Plum doubtfully, "but t'will make a fine ring." He had clipped off the tarnished silver bowl of the spoon and shaped the end of the handle onto a circle. Mr. Plum sized it to Jane's middle finger and then polished the ring until it gleamed.

"Why, Jane," said John, deeply touched. "Your Pea Ring. Thank you!" He took the ring from her and slipped it on his finger.

"Never take it off," Jane commanded sternly, "unless it is for the most important reason."

"And what would that be?" asked John as he gathered up his papers.

"You will know," answered Jane with the mysterious air she had perfected long ago. "It is yours now and you must use it as you will. And never fear, John. I shall help Mama. Perhaps the baby will be a little girl just like me!"

And John laughed aloud to think of a world in which two beings such as Jane might exist. They talked for a while. Then Jane kissed John good night on the forehead and padded away to her room with Winston at her heels. John pulled off his clothing and slipped a nightshirt over his head. He lay sleepless for a very long while. Truly he would miss his sister; they might look different, but in their hearts they were as alike as one person. Finally, tired and exhilarated at the same time, he slept. He dreamed of ships and silver rings and peas.

◇ ◇

Two days later the family and servants all gathered outside on the graveled drive. Jane stood close to her mother. David stood behind them both. John and his father would travel by coach to Plymouth and from there board the ship that would take them to Canada.

"We are off, Emma. Take care, my dear," said her husband with surprising tenderness. It was not the first time he had left his wife to bear a child alone. "Say farewell to your son."

"We said our goodbyes already, James. I do not believe in making a spectacle." John hugged his mother and she stiffly hugged him back.

"Goodbye, David," John said to his brother and they shook hands. "Take care of Brierly."

"Take care yourself, John," said David with great gusto.

"Where has Jane gone off to?" Lady Emma wondered, looking around the lawns and gardens that edged the house. "How could she be so cruel as to not say goodbye?"

"There is nothing to be done about it. We have no time to wait for her," said Lord MacNeil, hustling John into the carriage. "We must be away." And in moments the carriage was rolling down the drive. The horses pulled it through the ash wood, past the small lodge house, and through the open gate. And there was Jane, hanging from one side of the gate, waving wildly. John leaned out the window and blew her a kiss.

"Remember!" she shrieked. "Only for something very important!"

"1 shall!" shouted John. "And I will wait for your thoughts!"

"Good heavens!" mumbled Lord MacNeil. "The sooner that girl is married and this boy is away at sea the better." And he put all thoughts of his family out of his mind. Jane and Brierly disappeared in the trees, but John could feel them in his very soul. It would be a long while before he saw his home once more. The adventure had begun.

# CHAPTER
# TWO

All that day and into the late afternoon, the coach rolled down the rough dirt road that led along the sea to Plymouth. Each league carried John farther from Brierly and closer to the new life that awaited him. He began a letter to Jane. The carriage bumped and jostled his quill, and the ink bottle threatened to tip. John suspected that Jane would like the blotches on the page. They would make his journey seem more real to her.

*My dearest Jane,* he wrote, struggling to keep the letters even a little straight. *Father glares. The coach is small and stuffy. I must wear a wig, but I am the son of an officer and a peer and so must look the part. I am warm. It is like having a small cat ride on your head. Still, the canvas covers are thrown back from the coach windows and the sea air comes in. We will stop when night falls, and then start out again at dawn. Father wishes to waste no time in reaching Plymouth and the ship. I do believe we will spend the night at The Saucy Maiden. You know the establishment, I think. It is the*

*inn that Mama will barely look at when she passes by on*
*her way to Plymouth.*

The Saucy Maiden was a noisy, happy place, John
discovered, filled with sailors and other travelers. He and
his father took seats at a table. Red-faced servants carried
platters of food and drink to them through the crowded
room. Smoke from roasting meat and dozens of white
clay pipes clouded the air. Laughter rose and fell like
the tide. After John and his father had eaten, the land-
lord took them upstairs to their room. It was small but
clean. The windows were paned with watery glass that
looked out onto the ocean below.

"It is as crowded as the carriage," laughed John, looking about the room with its slanted ceiling and dark,
polished furnishings.

"This will seem like a ballroom once you have spent a
week in the cabin of a ship," said his father. "Come here,
John. I will show you something." He pulled a roll of
heavy paper from a leather document case and spread it
on a table.

"It is a map," said John with interest, leaning over the
table.

"A map of where duty will take us, much like those
maps that you will draw," his father replied, tracing a
route with his finger. They had talked of this on the way
to Plymouth. "To reach Canada is a long and complicated journey. It will take many months to come to our
final destination. First, you cross the ocean. That may
sound simple, but the weather can make it a voyage that

you will long remember. The ship will sail inland as far as the city of Quebec."

"Could we not sail to New York and go overland?" asked John.

"It is possible," answered his father. "But we will go up the St. Lawrence instead. I have dispatches for the military at Quebec."

John ran his hand across the land called Canada. How large this place was; all of England could fit in one of its corners.

"Here." His father pointed to the end of an oval shape. "Fort Niagara on Lake Ontario. We will attempt to reach it before winter. In all likelihood I shall go on with other dispatches and you will accompany me. Time alone will tell."

"It sounds so easy," mused John, straightening up.

"Hardly!" his father cautioned. He rolled the map and slid it back into the document case. "There is nothing easy about Canada or the colonies, John. You will learn that you must make your own judgments about these people and the best way to live among them. You will find that there are many opinions."

That night in bed, John added a bit more to his letter.

*Ask Mr. Walsh to show you the maps in the library, Jane. They are not recent maps. I will draw new ones and send some home as we travel, so you may see where we have gone. Still, the maps in the library will give you an idea of more or less where I am. We leave very early next morning and I must try to sleep now. Father says*

*that it will not do for me to fall asleep in the carriage.*
*My wig drops off. I do think I can feel you sending out*
*your thoughts to me tonight, Jane. Sleep well.*

The next day Lord MacNeil followed his son into the
carriage and rapped sharply on the roof, signaling
the driver to proceed.

"We are off!" he shouted, slapping his thighs. "We
will be in Plymouth by noon."

The carriage rolled along, fields of grain and vegetables in varied green rows on one side, the deep blue edge
of the English Channel on the other. They went through
small fishing villages with their draped nets drying in
the sunlight and rumbled past farms where sheep grazed
in soft, grassy meadows. Slowly the traffic grew more
crowded. Wagons and coaches, men on horseback, and
people on foot pulling carts and carrying baskets all
headed up and down each side of the road. The dirt
changed to cobbles. John leaned out the window. Beyond
the roofs of the houses and buildings he could see the
masts of ships pointing into the sky. The driver reined in
the sweat-flecked team. They had arrived.

◇ ◇

John quickly learned that there is nothing so busy as a
seaport. Ships came and went from everywhere in the
world. The docks were filled with cargo and an endless
tide of people shifting back and forth. Against the wharf
rested the *H.M.S. Amazon*. She would carry them to
Canada. Other warships and merchant sailing vessels

were anchored out in the sound. Sails were furled, and the British flag flew at many staffs. Here and there other pennants and flags rose and fell like hands in brightly colored gloves, waving hello or farewell. The ships swung lazily in the wind, their bows always searching for the breeze. Sweating, sun-browned sailors pulled on oars as launches went from ships to the wharves and back again. The *Amazon* was provisioned and many of the sailors were aboard. They would leave the next day with the outgoing tide.

Lord MacNeil led the way up the gangplank onto the deck of the ship. The skipper, Captain Blair, a very round man, stood there to greet them. Already sailors were racing to the carriage, unloading the small trunks and cases that had been carried from Brierly.

"Lord MacNeil, sir!" called Blair. "And this must be your son." He removed his tricorne hat and bowed with exaggerated courtesy. Lord MacNeil and John did the same.

"Blair, you rascal, you are stouter than ever!" laughed MacNeil. John stared at his father. Slowly he had watched him changing in the last days from the stiff, brittle man he had always known. Here his father seemed more relaxed, although he was no less gruff and demanding. This is his world, thought John. I have never known it, just as I have never really known him.

"Well, what do you think?" MacNeil strode down the deck. "Is this not all I said it would be?" John marveled at the change in his father. Away from Brierly and back on a ship, he glowed with life.

"It is wonderful," John answered. "I did not suppose the ship would be so large. And the sails! How do you keep track of them all?" He looked up at the heavy canvas furled and tied neatly on the yards. High above the deck, sailors checked rigging and tightened lines that secured the sails.

"One learns to do it, as you shall learn. Having a seaman's skills will serve you well," said his father and he scanned the deck for a moment. "Tom! Tom Apple!"

A giant of a man stomped over and touched his hand to his hat in a salute.

"Aye, sir," bellowed the giant.

"You look well, man. Ready for sea again?" Lord MacNeil shouted back, looking the giant up and down.

"Aye, sir, that I am," roared Apple.

Mercy, thought John, does no one speak here? They all shout. Jane would like it. She did love to scream down mossy wells to hear the echo.

"Are you ready to take on one more small task?" asked Lord MacNeil. Captain Blair chuckled.

"Ready and able, sir," yelled Apple. "If I can care for the sails on this ship, I can do anything." Tom Apple was an enormous man with heavy shoulders and large hands. He was the ship's boatswain. He supervised the men who mended the sails and he kept watch over the canvas and thread, needles, and palms, all the things needed for their work.

"You will keep one eye on the sails and your men, and the other on my son, John. He has not been to sea before, Tom. He needs a good teacher."

"That's that, then," roared Captain Blair. "Come below, sir, I wager you are dry." And the two men disappeared below decks. John turned to see Tom Apple watching him.

"So, you've never been to sea, have you?!" thundered Tom Apple. "I'll teach you all you need to be a fine seaman!" And he clapped John across the shoulder. John staggered a little and his wig and hat fell off. Tom picked up the wig and plopped it back on John's head rather crookedly. He handed him the hat.

"You must get rid of that thing," whispered Tom, pointing to the wig.

So he can speak in a normal voice, John thought. Aloud, he sighed. "No. Where I go the wig goes. Son of an officer and all that."

"Too bad," said Tom sympathetically. "But cheer up. Mayhap it will be lost at sea!"

"Maybe it will," John laughed.

They climbed down the companionway steps to the lower deck of the ship. John could smell tar and scrubbed wood and the scent of the men who berthed here. Tom Apple showed John the small aft cabin the boy would share with his father. He began John's education as they walked the narrow passage.

"There are many ranks on a ship and a hundred jobs," he said. "There is the captain and his officers. Then there is the master. The master, he navigates, finds our position, and sets the courses we sail. The quartermaster, he takes care of supplies. On the big ships, the surgeon takes care of our ailing bodies and the chaplain, bless him, takes care of our souls." He laughed loudly as he led John back onto the busy deck. "Wander around, my lad, and see what you will see."

John did so. The *Amazon* was a frigate. By the standards of the Royal Navy she was a rather small warship at 175 feet, but to John's young eyes she was enormous. The thirty guns she carried would be as deadly as those on a much larger vessel. He leaned his head back and peered upward. The *Amazon*'s three masts towered above him. Lines and rigging crisscrossed the deck in what he later would learn was a perfect pattern. John walked forward as far as he could go. He leaned over the bow of the ship and saw the face of a woman, the ship's figurehead. Her calm painted face gazed out at things only she could see.

"She's a fine lass, is she not!" Tom Apple called from behind him.

"Yes," answered John, although he wondered what his mother would think of the carving with its full, womanly figure and very little clothing.

"They say a woman's shape calms the stormiest sea," said Tom Apple, reading John's mind. He smiled at the lad's discomfort. Had he ever been so young himself?

"Does it work?" asked John, his cheeks flaming.

"No, but she looks nice, doesn't she?" laughed Tom and John laughed too.

The next day the *Amazon* bustled with activity as the crew of two hundred men prepared to sail that afternoon when the tide went out. Ships were moved by the wind, but a ship as large as the *Amazon* needed help when leaving its moorings. When the tide went out, pulling

the ⬚ e *Amazon*
as ⬚

the ⬚ . "When
the ⬚ own well
car ⬚

J ⬚ htly. His
ske ⬚ tools he
kep ⬚ of oiled
lea ⬚ side with
bre ⬚ on, not
a d ⬚ It had a
stra ⬚ walked.
He ⬚ vas well,
slap ⬚ hat atop
it al ⬚ the deck.

His father stood there with Captain Blair.

"Father, sir," said John and Lord MacNeil turned to his son. He was in full dress uniform as always.

"Yes, John. Ah, you do look fine, that wig quite suits you," answered Lord MacNeil, letting his eyes drift over his son.

"May I go ashore for a few hours, sir?" asked John.

"Do not stray too far from the ship," warned Captain Blair. "This is Plymouth Harbor after all, and the people here," he coughed discreetly, "are not the most genteel."

"Oh, I will take care," answered John in what he hoped was a convincing manner.

"Well then, go! And enjoy it, my son. You will not set foot on land for some time," said Lord MacNeil. John thanked his father and ran off down the gangplank.

He pulled off his hat, whipped off the hated wig, and tucked it under his belt. Putting his hat back on at a rakish angle, he joined the crowd that walked up and down the docks.

What a sight it was! The noise was great and the smells were endless. Fresh bread and grilling sausage competed with the odor of onions and potatoes dug up that day. Vendors had stalls set up against the tall, narrow buildings away from the water.

"What will you have, my fine boy?" shouted a man. "A boy such as yourself needs a good pistol!"

"Lemons and limes! Lemons and limes!" sang an old woman. "You cannot keep your teeth without lemons and limes." She smiled a toothless smile at John as he went by her stall.

A man going to sea for three years could find all he needed here. There was clothing and food, coconuts from the islands, and blood oranges from the south. Piles of fish, freshly caught that day, lay before the fishmonger. Hanging sides of beef drew flies, and noisy chickens clucked from wooden cages.

John sat down on a small keg and uncapped his document case. He pulled out a sheaf of papers and a stick of charcoal and began to draw. There were so many faces. He watched the river of sailors that ran both ways up and down the waterfront. Some had seabags flung across their backs. Others carried coils of rope or small kegs filled with sloshing liquid. He sketched for an hour, and with his quick strokes, Plymouth came to life on the paper.

Men and women moved in and out of the buildings.
Many of the places were taverns and their signs hung
above the open doors. The Wandering Sailor, The Rose
and Thistle, The Blue Boar, The Mermaid — that one
with a figurehead leaning out over the entrance — they
all did a brisk business. John stopped outside The
Mermaid. The smell of smoke and roasting pork drifted
into the street. Inside, serving girls swayed between the
tables carrying wide platters. Sailors laughed and someone played a fiddle. John stood in the street and looked
up at the mermaid that hung above him. Her blank
carved eyes stared out to sea. Long yellow hair curled
over her shoulders.

"He's in love!" roared a deep voice as a huge hand
slapped his back, nearly knocking him over. "Many a lad
has fallen in love with that one. I think it's safer to love
the sea itself!" And Tom Apple bellowed in laughter at
his own joke.

"I cannot be in love with her," said John. The best way
to deal with Tom, he had soon learned, was to rise to whatever salty bait was offered and answer a joke with a joke.

"And why would that be?" asked Tom, his eyes wide
with feigned innocence.

"I am already in love with the lady on the *Amazon*,"
explained John with a straight face. Tom laughed harder
than ever at that.

"You are not alone, lad. You are not alone."

John stuffed the paper and charcoal back into the
document case. He capped it and slung the case over his
shoulder.

They began to walk through the crowds, Tom leading and John following. The flow of people parted for officers with gold trim on their uniform coats and powdered wigs on their heads. It parted for big Tom Apple as well. Who would want to be knocked into the filthy harbor by such a giant?

"Time to go aboard," said Tom. "Only a few hours until the ebb tide goes out." He guided John ahead of him with a big hand, watchful of the passing sailors.

"I am ready," John said over his shoulder. "All my things are stowed." John pulled his wig from his pocket and set it back on his head under his hat as they approached the ship. His head began to grow warm beneath the miserable thing.

"All tidy?" asked Tom.

"All tidy," John answered. "Shipshape and Bristol fashion!" Tom had offered to teach him how to speak like a sailor.

"At least you will speak in the way a gentleman sailor would speak," Tom laughed, "Not like an old tar such as myself."

John now knew the names of the sails and the parts of the boat. In turn, John promised to show Tom Apple how to print his name. On the long voyage across the Atlantic, there would be time for that. Now the sailing of the *Amazon* was all that mattered. Like a great creature, restlessly leaning to the sea and her fate, she pulled, groaning, at her moorings.

Then the tide began to go out, and one by one the ships slowly, majestically, swung around on their moorings as though they could not bear the thought of yet once again leaving land and home.

"Stand by to cast off, Mr. Whip," said Captain Blair to the first officer.

"Stand by to cast off!" called the officer to the sailing master and he, in turn, shouted out the orders to the crew. One by one the heavy hawsers were loosened from the pilings. Seamen strained to fend the ship off from the wharf. Then the flow of the tide caught the *Amazon* and pulled her out away from the dock and into the harbor.

"Stand by to make sail, Mr. Whip," said the Captain, and in rapid succession each command was passed down from him to the others. Quickly the sails — the mainsail, the jibs, the mizzen sail — were unfurled by the men who clung to the yards and rigging by their toes. The sails filled with wind and, carried by the current and the steady breeze, the *Amazon* began to pick up speed. A sailor at the wheel expertly guided the ship through the channel, passing the other boats that still lay at anchor.

"Ahoy, *Amazon*!" called a voice behind them. John turned around. There, coming up fast on the port side, was a graceful sailing launch.

"Have an eye!" Tom Apple shouted to the launch. "What vessel are you?"

"The *Pod*," called the young man, who eased his sailboat closer to the *Amazon*. "Have you a John MacNeil on this ship?" His eyes scanned the decks.

"Aye, we do, and what would you want with young Mr. MacNeil?"

"I am John MacNeil!" called John, leaning over the side of the ship.

"I have a letter for you," called the young man. "'Tis from your sister." And he brought his boat very close to the hull of the *Amazon*. He stood and, holding his tiller steady with a bare brown foot, passed a sealed letter up to John, who stuffed it inside his coat. The young man flashed a white smile and bent to his vessel and home.

"Wait!" called John. He shrugged the document case from his shoulder and uncapped its end. Quickly he pulled papers from it and shuffled through until he found what he wanted.

"Make haste, my boy," laughed Tom Apple. "He cannot stand there all day!" But it seemed the young man could. John leaned far over the side and passed the letter into the sailor's fingertips.

"It is for Lady Jane MacNeil at Brierly!" shouted John. The young man was already making ready to turn his boat away. He brought it about and tacking into the breeze, skimmed back toward the landing. He waved once and then turned away.

"And what was all that?" asked Lord MacNeil, who had come up behind them.

"A letter from Jane!" laughed John and Lord MacNeil smiled slightly. They were close those two, he thought, perhaps too close. Distance would do them both good.

"Well, I am certain she has written a very long letter. After all, it has been nearly four days since we last saw her and Brierly. Who can say what has happened there in that time?"

But John's happiness was not affected at all by his father's remarks. He would read the letter later. Now too much was happening and John was caught up in the excitement that overtakes a vessel when she returns to the sea. It was not until later, when they reached the open waters of the English Channel and the ship was well underway, that the flurry of activity settled into the pattern it would hold for weeks.

John went to the stern of the *Amazon* where Captain Blair stood and watched England fade into the distance. The clear view of the shore blurred into hazy purples and greys. He felt an ache in his chest. He was a practical boy and had learned to shield himself from his brother's taunting, his mother's distracted air, and his father's distance. Like Jane, he held his most tender feelings deep inside and he did not often give in to them. This must be homesickness, he thought, and he knew that he missed more than Jane.

"Have ye been to sea before, sir?" asked the seaman who steered the ship. He watched John's face and knew what the young gentleman was feeling. He himself had suffered terribly from homesickness the first time he went to sea at eight years of age.

"No, I have not," answered John. He felt the words catch in his throat.

"Well, 'tis a hard life, but a grand one," the seaman said. "Ye will see things ye would never have seen if ye stayed at home." His hands rested lightly on the *Amazon*'s huge wheel. Now and again he glanced at the compass.

"May I try that?" asked John. The sailor looked over at Captain Blair, who nodded his approval. Helming the ship in this steady wind and light seas was just the thing to take the mind off of homesickness.

"South southwest. 'Tis here on the compass. See the star ahead just coming out? Ye can sail by that as well, for a wee bit. Then ye pick another star."

John set his hands on the wheel. He felt the pull of the ship's rudder and the sea that ran beneath it. "She feels alive," he wondered, and the Captain smiled to himself as he went below to dine with the officers.

Later that night after a quick meal of cold meat and more or less fresh bread, John lay on his berth and tore open Jane's letter. There was his sister's careful, familiar hand.

*My dear John,* she began. *Picture me settled on the bed in your room. Winston is here beside me. He is chewing one of your slippers, but not so badly that you will not be able to wear it again. I will write all my letters to you in this place when I am home. I already miss you dreadfully. Mama wanders in the garden and sighs. She sends her love to you and Father, but she does not have the strength to write. She says that she will begin a letter soon. David is crowing as though he is a lord of the land. I put a snake in his bed this afternoon, and I expect to hear his crowing change to a rather different sound any time now. You know how he detests snakes. Mary says she hopes you do not fall off the ship and drown. I know you will not.*

*It was Mr. Plum's nephew who carried this letter. I congratulated Mr. Plum at being so very clever to think of such a thing. Last night I sent out my thoughts to you. I told you to make certain to send back an answer soon.*

*Next week I am to have an adventurous outing of sorts. It is more exciting than dinner with Lord Elgie and even better than catching snakes for David's bed. We are to travel to London and stay for a month with Mama's friend, Lady Whiteson. I may be presented at Court! Do not laugh. I will behave for Mama's sake, although it would be fun to try out some of Lord Elgie's habits.*

*Good night, dear John. I must hurry to my room and lock myself in with Winston. I have just heard the most horrible noises coming from down the hallway in the direction of David's quarters.*

John laughed out loud. He folded the letter and put it under his pillow. Lord MacNeil sat across the small room at a desk. John knew that his father was too proud and stiff to ask, so he explained.

"They are well and Mama sends her love. She will write soon. It seems they will all go to London for a month. Jane is to be presented at Court." John yawned and lay down, pulling the blanket up over his shoulders. Exhausted by the day's activities, he was asleep in a moment.

"London," whispered Lord MacNeil in horror. "God save the King!"

# CHAPTER
# THREE

The strange thing about a ship is that given enough time, it ceases to be a ship at all. It becomes a world unto itself. Once you are out of sight of land, once you become accustomed to the slow movement of the deck beneath your feet, you forget what it is like to walk on something that does not have a life of its own. Out on the ocean, trees and flowered meadows barely seem real at all. Busy shops, barns filled with golden hay, churches edged with stones piled into walls, those things fade away like fog lifting at dawn on the water.

"The only thing that matters is the wind," Tom Apple told him. "Everything a sailor does on a ship is decided by the wind." The set of the sails, the angle of the deck, even the way John held his body all depended on how the wind behaved that day.

Seasickness did not bother John, which surprised Lord MacNeil. The boy wandered the ship, helping where he could, poking about and picking up bits of knowledge as he went. His cheeks grew brown. His arms and shoulders began to fill out with the work he did.

Sometimes John would go below and help the cook. Mr. Carroll was a happy man who was as much the ruler of his galley as Captain Blair was of the ship and certainly as respected as the captain himself. Mr. Carroll guarded the food with an eagle eye. The limes and bread that swung above his head in mesh netting were more precious than gems of emerald or topaz. He seemed to be the only man on board whose life and work were not driven by the ocean.

"They have to eat," he said to John. "Fine seas or squalls, hurricanes or typhoons, rough or flat, they have to eat." And so he would supervise the mess cooks and boys in preparing the endless rounds of meals for the crew.

On Tuesday, Thursday, Saturday, and Sunday it was salt pork or beef. Cheese and butter were served the other days. There would be fresh vegetables, turnips, potatoes, and yams only for as long as they lasted, then dried peas and pickled cabbage would take their place. It was boring food, and yet after a day of sailing, the sailors' appetites were sharpened by the sea air and they ate with relish. Even the plainest of meals seemed a warm comfort.

As the son of Lord MacNeil, John took his meals with his father and the other officers. Captain Blair did not eat alone as many skippers did. He enjoyed the company of others far too much. Dinner at his table was a small island of English tradition and culture in the very rough waters of the British Navy. Mr. Carroll would stand at the door of the wardroom glowering at the sailors who brought in the covered dishes. The table was always laid with clean white linen. Candlelight flickered on the captain's own silver that was set near the pewter plates on which the meal was served. There was no salt pork or pickled cabbage on this table. Each officer, including Lord MacNeil, had sent on board his own choice rations.

*The wide ocean of difference between officer and crew is not just a matter of rank,* John wrote to his sister. *There are two worlds here. The seamen are like the common people back home — the poor people, the farmers, and the fishermen. The officers are the rulers. You cannot break rules here, Jane. The punishment is terrible.*

It was a hard life for these sailors. They worked and stood watch no matter what the weather. John did not have to do the worst of tasks, but he tried almost all of them. Lord MacNeil watched in despair in those first few weeks as his son slipped on the deck and fumbled with lines. But gradually John's hands became callused. He held his brushes and quills with a new strength. He learned that the first star rising in the night to glitter above you as you steered the ship was more precious than the finest jewel. To roll into his bunk at the end of the day and fall into the dreamless sleep of well-earned exhaustion was a sweet pleasure.

Lord MacNeil was often below deck or in conversation with Captain Blair. John spent much of his time under Tom Apple's wing and as the days passed, he slowly came to love the sea. It was a feeling John would have for the rest of his life. It had nothing to do with

Tom Apple's endless lessons or the work he helped do on the *Amazon*. He simply woke one morning and felt himself part of the ship. That was a comfort, for his homesickness faded slowly. Sometimes he expected to hear the clicking of Winston's claws and the patter of Jane's bare feet coming down the companionway to his cabin. He often looked down at her Pea Ring and wondered what his sister was doing. He thought of how Jane would enjoy all of this. He would share it with her the only way he could, and so he drew.

"Will you pose for me, sir?" he asked the first officer, Mr. Whip. Mr. Whip was standing on the poop deck looking very stately.

"Why, of course, my boy!" he answered and, puffing out his chest, looked statelier than ever.

John did portraits of all the officers. He sketched seamen straining at the wheel, sinewy arms and hard hands holding the ship on course. He drew men scrubbing the decks, their broad backs flexing under the plain shirts they wore.

*They spread a sand called slurry on the boards,* John wrote his sister. *Then on their hands and knees, they rub the slurry across the deck with sandstones. 'Holy stones' they call them, because they are the size and shape of bibles. The servants at Brierly would not like to scrub a kitchen floor in that way, Jane!*

The weather was fine. Even seas carried the *Amazon*, and she left a creamy trail of froth behind her. The winds were steady, and most days every inch of canvas could be flown. England's flag streamed out as the ship sped to Canada across the Atlantic.

"It is a remarkably easy passage," said Captain Blair one night at dinner. The meal had been cleared away. Officers sat with goblets of port, smoking their long, white clay pipes. The soft, measured creaking of rigging was a steady sound beyond the talk.

"You should not speak so soon, sir," advised Lord MacNeil. "We have been out for only three weeks. The sea is unpredictable — who can say what might blow up?"

"True, sir," mused the captain, and he looked at John. "We have all seen it happen in an instant. There will be a fine fluff of clouds in the distance. All your sails are full and you are moving along nicely, then it changes." He nodded in silence.

"How, sir?" asked John. He felt he needed a particularly hair-raising entry for his letter tonight. He was not disappointed at the captain's stories.

That evening, as the ship rolled gently beneath him, tucked into his berth, John wrote:

*Captain Blair said that he has experienced seas of more than forty feet. You cannot see an inch before you and men must be tied to the ship somehow, or else be washed overboard. The wind screams in the rigging and sails must be brought in. It is a hard thing to send brave men aloft for the job, but it is that or sink.*

He could imagine Jane reading this passage aloud in the nursery. Poor Mary! She would not sleep for a month after hearing such stories. Jane would lie awake in excitement picturing it all.

For the rest of the week John scanned the horizon. Each cloud was suspicious. Each wave that passed the ship, each puff of wind made him wonder whether it would bring a storm. But no truly foul weather arose. There were a few squalls. Lightning snapped above them, low thunder rumbled, and the ship sped along, driven by the hard wind and the huge, foam-spattered seas. Pelting rain washed the crusted salt from the *Amazon*'s decks and rigging.

"This is nothing!" roared the captain, who seemed to enjoy the heavy weather. Soaked to the skin, John was not so sure.

"At least there will not be such storms on the lakes, sir. Lake Erie especially is so small it must be like a pond," he said to his father as they dried themselves off in their cabin after one such event.

"It may be a lake, John, but all who have sailed it talk of dangerous weather that comes up suddenly. Believe me, it will have storms of its own. They say it is like a freshwater sea."

John thought of the chart in his father's cabin. How could such a small lake compare to the Atlantic? In time, perhaps, he would learn for himself.

In the days and weeks that passed, John felt the movement of the ship sift slowly into his blood. It became one with the steady beating of his heart. The creaking of rigging, the call of the watch, and the even, slow lift of waves were the things by which he now marked his life. Nearly two months passed. Then one morning, unable to sleep any longer, he rose and went on deck to watch the sun lift from the ocean in the east.

"Land ho!" called a seaman from the yards far above the deck. "Land ho!"

John squinted into the pale morning light. In the distance lay something softer than the line of the horizon, something as indistinct as a dream of a far-off place. Men were coming up on deck. His father, strangely bareheaded without his ever-present wig, shrugged into his coat as he came to the rail. Lord MacNeil peered into the distance, his eyes narrowing.

"I think I can see something," said John carefully, "but I cannot be certain." Captain Blair came up beside them. His eyes measured John for a moment.

"Go aloft then," he laughed. "You will see it clearly there, I wager." John looked up into the sky. Far above the deck, a sailor stood braced against the mast. He glanced at his father who said nothing, but watched him closely.

"Aye, sir!" cried John snappily, and he hurried to the ratlines that angled from the rail to the mast high above the deck. He held onto the rough rope and pulled himself up to the first rung. The ratlines were like rope ladders that the seamen used to climb into the rigging. Like a ladder except that it moves, thought John, but he had started up and could not stop now. His foot slipped once, but he held tightly to the lines.

"That's it, lad!" bellowed Tom Apple. "You're a true sailor now!"

Wakened by the commotion and noise on the top-sides, officers and seaman had come on deck. Some eyes looked out to sea; the first sight of land was always a welcome one. Below him, other sun-browned faces turned upward to watch his scrambling. He could hear cheers of encouragement. Then he was at the platform where the yard and its billowing sail crossed the mast. The seaman who stood there held out a hand and helped him up.

"Hold tightly, sir," the sailor advised, for the roll and sway of the ship could truly be felt this high in the air. The cold wind was stronger, too. It whipped John's hair back from his forehead and molded his shirt to his chest.

"Where is it?" he asked. "Where is land?" But then he saw. There it was to the west, mist-shrouded and mysterious to his eyes.

They had reached Canada.

❖ ❖

For the next weeks the *Amazon* followed the heartless footsteps of the British army at war. There was a harsh, chilling voyage up the St. Lawrence River to Quebec, which lay crushed under the heel of the British forces who now held it for England. The price had been high. Both commanders, General Wolfe and General Montcalm, were dead, lost in the battle with so many others from each side. Lord MacNeil spent his time with the British officers, but John remained aboard the

*Amazon* much of the time, not caring to see the marks of war all around the city of Quebec. As the days passed, he knew that soon his life on this ship would be ended. A month after they arrived, John said farewell to Tom Apple who would stay with the *Amazon*.

"Take care, my boy," Tom said. "'Tis a wild place you go to." He had become rather fond of John, who, as promised, had taught him how to print his name. John's last view of Tom Apple was of him striding off to a shabby tavern that had been much damaged in the battle. There he planned to dazzle the locals with his ability to write the two words in shaky letters. Tom. Apple.

With a party of men and Natives, John and his father pressed on to Montreal with dispatches from the military in Quebec. Led by General Jeffery Amherst, the British army had marched on the city earlier that spring. By September the French surrendered and Montreal was in English hands. From that city they were ordered on to Fort Niagara with Major Robert Rogers and yet more dispatches from Amherst.

"Is it to be war everywhere?" John asked his father as they left for Niagara on a soft, sunlit morning. "We have seen little else." John felt himself hardening against it all; the images he drew these last weeks were sad and cruel. Ravaged buildings, burned churches, wounded soldiers, and blank-faced families left with nothing, these pictures he sketched and then crumpled and tossed into the fire each night. He was unwilling to let such things live on by his hand. John had known the grim face of war to be horrible, but army against army was one thing; the razed homesteads and tales of horrors up and down the rivers were another.

"I think not," his father answered. Lord MacNeil had as little taste for it all as his son, but he could not let his feelings show. He must stand by the Crown whatever happened. "Only Detroit remains to be taken, and if Rogers and his men cannot do that, then no one can. In time the Crown will wisely and fairly rule a peaceful place here."

John said nothing to this. Surely his father was correct. The war was all but over and nothing like it would ever happen here again.

## CHAPTER
## FOUR

John stood looking down at the Niagara River. The warm spring sunshine felt wonderful on his back and shoulders as he watched the powerful current rush to Lake Ontario. Trees were already covered in pale green leaves, and birdsong filled the air each morning. A cool wind had come up from the water, so he held tightly to the sheet of paper on which he had been drawing the river. Soon he would add new maps to those he had already drawn since his arrival in Canada. Although it seemed to John that he had been here at Fort Niagara forever, their stay nearly was over. They would be leaving tomorrow on the next leg of their journey.

John felt excitement at this thought. They had made good time to Fort Niagara last fall, traveling with Major Rogers and the green-clad Rangers, a company of battle-seasoned colonial soldiers. The Major and those men had carried on to Fort Detroit, the last French stronghold. Lord MacNeil remained behind. It had not been an easy decision, but he had given his word to his wife, Lady Emma. John would come no closer to war than he had to.

Detroit's surrender came quickly, but by then it was December. Lord MacNeil and his party had to delay their journey to Detroit until the spring. Once the brutal winter closed in around Niagara, John felt himself become marooned in the fort as though on a desolate island of ice and snow.

It was a mild winter, they all said. How lucky we are. Yet John had experienced nothing like it before. In spite of heavy woolen blankets, he shivered each night. No fire could keep the stone-walled rooms truly warm. The sun barely rose in the sky each day and snowstorms marched in wind-driven lines across the gray landscape. Lake Ontario, over which the fort looked, was rimmed with ice. On quiet nights he could hear the groaning of ice shelves as pressure cracks raced across their frozen depths. But spring did come, a slow, creeping hint of changing light and weather. The ice broke into floes that the wind blew away. Bateaux, the flat-bottomed wooden vessels used on the lake, once again swung free.

John turned from the river. Lord MacNeil stood near the officers' quarters in conversation with two of the men who might accompany them. The clothing the men wore was travel-stained. Their faces were lean and hard. In contrast, his father looked as though he had stepped from a drawing room. John walked over to them.

"You must decide, scouts," ordered Lord MacNeil. "Are you coming with us?"

John watched the men as they weighed their choices.

"We be guides, Captain, not scouts," said Wallace Doig quietly.

"I know that, man," Lord MacNeil answered impatiently. "But guides or scouts, you must make up your minds."

"We need a wee bit of time to think on it," Wallace said. He was a careful man. It was his habit. He did not take a shot at a fleeing deer without carefully measuring the distance and the likelihood of a clean kill. He did not throw himself into events as some did, to be caught up and carried away like driftwood on the St. Lawrence River. He took his time and made his judgments.

"As you will, then," said Lord MacNeil. "We leave in the morning." He left the men to their decision and strode off to the officers' quarters.

"Will you come with us?" John asked Wallace. He liked the Scot and his Odawa companion, Natka. John had spent time with them each day since they had arrived at the fort a few weeks ago. They had patiently answered John's questions and told him stories of their lives on the frontier.

"Perhaps," answered Wallace, settling his musket across his lap as he and Natka both crouched on the ground to think. "A long walk on a fine spring day might be just what we need."

Wallace pulled from his head the felt bonnet with which no Scot went without. Wiping his brow, he ran thick fingers through his gray-flecked beard and hair. His woolen kilt shifted against his legs. With the return of spring, he again wore the clothing of the highlands.

On the coldest days here in this country he might lower himself to wear breeches. A kilt was the best, though, and much healthier. Of this he was convinced.

Wallace replaced his bonnet, cocking it just so. He weighed the opportunity he had been offered.

"I would much enjoy your company," said John. "And you would see your sons again." Wallace's wife, his Miami bride, Salla, had been the love of his life. She had died from a fever many years ago and he had never married again. Three sons, his "wee lads," were all he had left of her now. A simple campfire, his wee dear sons, and the wilderness around a man, that was the way to live.

The Scot smiled at the boy's openness. "Well, 'tis a long enough journey to Fort Detroit and good company does make the trail seem more pleasant," Wallace said thoughtfully.

"Do we go with them?" asked Natka. "It might be interesting."

John looked over at the man. Natka was an Odawa who from his youth had taken up the wandering life. He was tall and well muscled. His head was shaved halfway back, and his long black hair was drawn into a club tied with beaded thongs. John was fascinated by the blue tattoos that ran in geometric patterns across Natka's high forehead and along his face. He was also heavily tattooed on his arms and torso. He had thrust wide silver bracelets high up on each of his biceps over his full-sleeved shirt. His ears were pierced, and heavy silver earrings dangled from stretched earlobes. A breech cloth lightly studded with trade silver, leather leggings, and moccasins completed his outfit.

"Interesting, old friend?" wondered Wallace in his Scots burr. "To voyage across the lakes and country when we hear rumblings of unrest amongst the tribes, that is your idea of interesting?"

"People are hungry for trade goods," answered Natka, picking up his musket as he rose to his feet. "They ask themselves, how can the English take our lands by defeating the French in war? Where are the powder and balls we used to trade for with the French? I ask myself the same thing."

Wallace had heard the whisperings. With the British in power and in control of the fur trade, there were rumors that they now held a growing stranglehold on goods. The tribes could not hunt without guns and ammunition. Only a few used the old ways; spears and arrows were a thing of the past. He stood up, wincing at the creaking of his bones. Neither he nor Natka were young men anymore. Oh, they had been young once, full of energy, eager to explore the uncharted lands to the west. It was how they met, two young men out to see the world. But times were changing. An old man of forty-one should not be ranging around the countryside like this. Natka's voice interrupted his thoughts.

"We will go with you," Natka said to John, and Wallace nodded his agreement.

"I shall tell my father," John said in excitement.

"We hav'na seen that part of the country for a wee bit," added Wallace. "It will be good to head home." He, too, glanced at John. The lad had an eagerness about him that did not seem English at all.

"It will be interesting," said Natka, and Wallace laughed, shaking his head.

"I look forward to Fort Detroit," John said to Wallace.

"Out there it isna civilized like this, lad," the Scot told John. "It'll make Niagara seem like a palace."

John wondered at men who could call Niagara a palace. True, the large stone building, constructed by the French as a trading post, was more imposing than any he had seen on the lakes. But despite its many fireplaces, the stone walls and floors held a constant chill.

"Well, it will be interesting," said John, and Wallace roared with laughter.

"Aye! That it will be!" The two men waved to John, then with Wallace still chuckling, went to the trading room for provisions. They would then move on to the magazine for powder, balls, and shot. John hurried over to the stone house where his father would likely be with the fort's commander. He crossed the entranceway and climbed the staircase to the second floor. Although the door to Major Walters's rooms was open, John cleared his throat so that he might be noticed.

"Come in, John," invited Major Walters, who sat across from Lord MacNeil at a polished oak table.

"Good afternoon, Major Walters, sir," said John. Then he turned to his father. "Excuse me, sir, but I am pleased to say that they will come with us." Lord MacNeil nodded. He was not really surprised at his son's pleasure. He had noted John's slowly growing friendship with the men and the boy's interest in everything they told him.

"And who is that?" asked Major Walters curiously.

"The Odawa called Natka and Wallace Doig the Scot," offered John.

"Ah, yes," nodded Major Walters. "Most interesting men."

John struggled to keep the grin from his face.

"They have traveled far to the north and west," Lord MacNeil told him. "They know this land and the people well. Doig has made his home on Lake Erie. It seems he has a vessel there."

"A ship? There are no ships above the Falls," said Major Walters.

"Wallace has a boat he built himself," said John. "It is as you told me, Father. This place is filled with surprises."

"Well, there may be no British ships, although there soon will be," said Major Walters firmly. "We shall build more bateaux. His Majesty's ships, *Huron* and *Michigan*, shall be constructed. There will be a British naval presence on Lake Erie in no time, or I will know why."

"Until then it will be bateaux and canoes," said John's father. "We will make good speed." John had heard from Wallace that traders could reach Detroit in ten days. Did they not sleep? he wondered.

John drifted around the room, watching and listening, seemingly forgotten by the two officers for a moment. He had discovered that he had as much a talent for it as Jane. He was well enough liked, but in general he was ignored. He learned many things this way and it also let him carefully observe the faces he would later draw.

"You will take six soldiers of the 60th with you, Captain," Major Walters was saying. "They will be armed as usual and, although we are short of supplies here, reasonably provisioned. They shall serve as replacements at Detroit. The escort that accompanied you from Montreal will remain here." He poured a cup of port for himself and offered one to John's father. Lord MacNeil declined.

"We expect to live off the land, sir. They say there is much game."

"Easily done," said Walters, leaning back in his chair. "You shall have a dozen Senecas as well, and those two scouts, pardon me, guides I hear they prefer, to accompany you. Bateaux in the beginning. Canoes wait for you upriver at the Carrying Place. I suspect you will find Detroit somewhat more British now. Rogers had little difficulty convincing them to surrender last year." Walters leaned back and watched the firelight glitter across the dark surface of the port.

"A good number for the party, sir," observed Lord MacNeil. It would be enough men to see them all safely there, and yet not so many to make the journey a slow one.

"And one more shall be added to it," said Walters briskly.

"Sir?"

"Lieutenant Lindsay will accompany you."

John stifled a groan as he left his father and Major
Walters to their talk. He clattered down the steps,
through the shadowy vestibule, and out into the yard. It
would have to be Lindsay! Lieutenant Lindsay had been
in Canada since the beginning of the war with France.
He had come down the St. Lawrence River with them
as part of the escort from Montreal. Although he had
not ever said so, John had good reason to believe that
Lindsay did not share his own keen interest in the
country. There had been several polite disagreements
that ended in silence. Lindsay was a young man who
took a very serious view of things indeed. Humorless
and crisp, he was utterly devoted to his duties as an officer. Well, John would not let Lindsay spoil the prospects
of this trip.

John passed red-coated soldiers who were going about
their business and stopped near the edge of the bluff,
looking up the Niagara River. The current was strong
even here, but two leagues up it was truly powerful. That
was as far as they would go by bateaux, to what everyone
called the Carrying Place. From that point, you had to
portage, carrying your goods and canoes overland along
the ever-steepening walls of the river and past the Falls
themselves.

"Ah, a romantic," called Wallace who had come up
behind John. "Of what do you dream, lad?" He looked
over the river that ran below them.

"Nothing," laughed John, looking up at him and
Natka, who stood nearby. "I only wonder about the

Falls. We came here so quickly last year and did not stop to view them. I might have gone myself but for the weather. Are they as grand as everyone says?"

"Like nothing you've ever seen in your life, lad. I leave it at that and let you judge for yourself." And with Natka beside him, he walked away to see to his last affairs. Lord MacNeil emerged from the stone building and strode toward John, glancing at Wallace and Natka as they passed by.

"I suspect that you will get to know those two even better before this is all over," he said to his son. "There is much they can teach you. They understand this land in a way we do not. Learn from them, John. Between the pair they speak French, English, and, most importantly, Odawa. That Natka most likely speaks other dialects. You must have interpreters here."

"We will have more men than we supposed," said John, knowing what reaction would come. He watched his father's face grow red with irritation.

"I know what you are thinking and you will keep it inside your head," Lord MacNeil demanded.

"I said nothing," remarked John innocently to his father, who braced himself and stood gazing over the river with his hands clasped behind his back.

"You did not need to. I could sense your feelings even as you left the room back there. Jeffrey Lindsay is a good man, John. A trifle stiff, I suppose." John thought this a remarkable comment coming from someone as stiff as his father. "But his unfailing duty to the Crown and his ability to command may not be questioned."

"I did not think to question them, Father. It is just that I am certain he does not care for me or, in fact, anything in Canada. Something about the way he looks down his nose at it all." John leaned back his head and struck a serious pose, eyebrows slightly lifted, the corners of his mouth turned down. Lord MacNeil forced himself not to smile.

"Yes, well, we shall excuse that, I believe, since the orders come from General Amherst, and orders from the Commander of the British forces cannot be ignored. Besides that, he is the nephew of one of Amherst's friends in England. Connections speak loudly here as everywhere, my boy."

John picked up a pebble and tossed it over the wall toward the river far below. Jane would have been leaning so far over, he thought, she might have tumbled off. Lindsay was already far from his mind.

"Pack your gear then, John. We leave at sunrise." How distractible the boy was.

"Yes, sir," John called to his father as Lord MacNeil left him and turned to other business. John hurried to the stone house. A year ago, departing at such an early hour would have seemed harsh to John, but now he woke each day at dawn with no effort. He could stow his gear quickly. He no longer fell from horseback; he had spent many days carefully guiding a mount through woods and meadows. He paddled a canoe with growing skill. He might often be ignored, but he felt comfortable with the rugged men, the Natives and traders, as well as the officers. In the last months this wild country had slowly begun to work its changes upon him.

Inside the room, John quickly packed his belongings. He brought out his document case. It now held the maps he had drawn for his father and the Crown, as well as his own papers. Its contents changed often as he slipped in new drawings of the things he saw. He had sent two thick envelopes to England filled with letters and sketches for Jane. In return, he had received one very long letter from her; it had come with the endless military dispatches and a letter from his mother for his father. John sat on his narrow bed, smoothed open the paper, and reread Jane's sentences with pleasure. It was almost as if he could hear her clear voice speaking to him. It was no wonder she came into his mind so often.

*Dearest John*, she began. *It seems as though you have been gone for years. Winston is heartbroken. He eases his pains by chewing what is left of your slippers. I promise I shall purchase you a new pair before you return home. You would not care to wear these.*

*I have been to London with Mama and I went to Court. It was very grand and for days I felt grand as well. I am too young to have been formally presented, but I was introduced to His Highness Prince George at a garden party held at a house in the country nearby. With the new baby on the way, Mama did not really wish to go out in public, but Prince George's mama, Princess Augusta, insisted. She loves babies and ladies who are having babies. They say she hopes for a dozen grandchildren when Prince George marries.*

*The most amazing thing is who I met there, John. As I strolled through the garden, peering this way and that — you know how hard it is for me to see faces — I walked straight into a young man. I spilled a glass of punch all down his waistcoat and he dropped cake with butter-cream icing on the shoulder of my gown. Apologies were wasted, so we introduced ourselves. Mama said later that I was most forward. A young lady of gentle breeding should be introduced properly.*

*He is young Viscount Henry Fitzwalter, a most distant cousin many times removed of His Highness Prince George. Mama says that Henry is favored by Prince George because he has no ambitions to the Crown. He is behind hundreds of others in line, I believe. It would he quite a wait, would it not? Henry says that he and the Prince get along well because they got into so much mischief together when they were boys.*

*And yes, we are Henry and Jane since we became friends instantly. He is like you in some ways. He draws wonderfully and he knows many things about plants and animals and birds, but I think he is a little like me as well. He wears spectacles. He cannot see without them. I insisted that Mama take me to a shop where a clever man makes them. I now own a pair of spectacles. I did have to swear never to put them on in public, but now and again I slip them out of my bag and peek through them.*

*I am to have tea with Prince George and his mama, Princess Augusta, next week. Henry will be there as well, of course. I have not decided whether I shall wear*

*the spectacles. It would be nice to see the royal faces as*
*something other than royal blurs. Besides, what if I spill*
*tea on the future King of England?*

John had read the letter many times. It was good that
Jane now had a confidant. Winston was grand company,
but Jane needed another person with whom to share her
ideas. Winston seldom did more than grunt and roll over
when you asked him for his opinions. How fine it would
be to have the same thing for himself; perhaps a friend
waited for him somewhere in the wilderness. Shrugging
off such nonsense, he read on.

Jane went on about the household at Brierly, how
Mary was preparing the nursery for the new baby that
would be born that fall. It was now the following spring.
How strange to think that the baby had been born many
months ago and that he now had a new sister or brother.
Lord MacNeil did not speak of it at all. Childbirth was a
dangerous thing for women. No matter how strong
they were, they sometimes did not survive. John refused
to think of such possibilities. Perhaps a new letter would
arrive to relieve the worry that nagged even at the back
of his mind.

But before any dispatch cases were delivered to Fort
Niagara, before the sun was even well into the sky the
next morning, they were gone. It was as Lord MacNeil
had predicted months ago: from Fort Niagara, he would
likely be sent out even farther now that Canada was
England's. It was on to Lake Erie and up the Detroit
River. Fort Detroit, their next destination, lay hundreds

of miles away. Lord MacNeil would carry news from Niagara and Albany and then remain to serve there under Captain Campbell. And at Fort Detroit, John was certain, their lives would settle into a quiet routine at last.

---⬦---

# CHAPTER
# FIVE

For the next weeks they traveled. At first it was easy as
the men poled the thirty-foot bateaux up the Niagara
River. Then, as they neared the Falls and made a landing
at the Carrying Place, there was the inevitable portage.
The three large canoes that waited for them, as well as
their supplies, had to be carried far upstream around the
Falls by horses and carts, which would later be sent back.

The portage was not so far, perhaps another two
leagues, but it would be all uphill. The soldiers and the
Senecas loaded their supplies into the carts that stood
by the river. They would carry the light birchbark canoes
themselves. Everyone, except Lord MacNeil and Lieutenant Lindsay, shared the burden of the gear. Even
John, in spite of Lindsay's elegant stare of disapproval,
slung a heavy pack over his shoulders. He was soon
soaked in sweat. John pulled off his hot, itchy wig and
tucked it under his belt. Lord MacNeil said nothing.
The fact that his son was beginning to cast off some
of the conventions of England was slowly ceasing to
surprise him. Canada seemed to have that effect on some

people. Lindsay, fresh and scarcely breathing hard, wiped a slight dampness from his brow and kept his opinions to himself.

All were armed, including John, who carried a musket, powder horn, and shot. He had not wanted even that, but his father had insisted. To John's eyes, Wallace and Natka were armed as though they were going into battle. They had told him many times of the dangerous men an unsuspecting traveler might meet. Each carried muskets, knives, and tomahawks.

"You never can tell," said Wallace, as they walked along. "Take care, lad. Keep your powder and your musket dry and you will do well."

"I am a terrible shot," John confessed in a whisper.

"We shall remedy that in time," said Wallace. "Look." He pointed into the sky. A trembling cloud of mist hung in the air. John realized he could hear a strange, low rumbling. On the clearest days he had seen that same mist many times from Fort Niagara, even though the Falls were leagues away.

"They say men use that mist as a landmark," said John, shifting his pack so it rode more comfortably. They all fell into silence as they came closer to the Falls. The thundering grew louder. Droplets carried by the wind fell in a softly shining rain all around them.

Then the trees cleared and John could see where the Niagara River poured itself into a deep gorge, flowing over the lip with an unending roar. It was a deep blue-green and the sight of it somehow made him feel uncomfortable. Seagulls drifted in the updrafts. An eerie rainbow floated above it all. John spotted a branch bobbing up and down in the water. It floated to the edge of the Falls and in a moment it was swept over.

"No man nor canoe could survive that," observed Lord MacNeil.

"Who would ever be foolish enough to try?" Lindsay said dryly. Since they had left that morning he had been silent. John would have talked, but the young officer kept to himself. Lindsay wiped the back of his hand across his forehead. With his red eyebrows and pale skin, the sun was not kind to him.

"There are fools everywhere," answered Lord MacNeil.

Once high beyond the Falls and the tremendous pull of the river, the canoes were lowered into the water. Packs were evenly distributed and each person picked up a paddle. Their days took on a pattern of mindless stroking. Sometimes the sun shone brightly and sweat rolled down their faces as they kept a steady rhythm. Once or twice it rained. John watched herons stalk frogs or small fish along the riverbanks. Lines of geese fluttered in the mist down to the water. Drops pattered on the birchbark canoes and the surface of the river. Rings of ripples overlapped in the water.

Each night they camped. They pulled the canoes up near the shore and unloaded. Carried away from the water, the canoes were turned on their sides to make shelters against the damp for those who would sleep outside. Tents were pitched. Fires were lit and someone would set up a tripod of branches to hold the iron cooking pot. Sometimes the soldiers shot at the ducks that landed on the river each evening. Natka might spear fish, standing poised against the sunset like a statue until he let his spear fly. He would gut his catch and run a green stick through it, then broil it over the fire. There was so much game, fish, fowl, deer, rabbits, and bear that John felt certain people here would never go hungry.

As the days went by, the weather warmed. Lord MacNeil remained fully dressed, a wig and tricorne hat upon his head. Lindsay did the same. The soldiers removed their coats and packed them away. John went in shirtsleeves, although he wore his tricorne as protection against the sun. He tucked the wig into his belongings — he would wear it again, although he was not certain when. To his surprise, his father said nothing about the casual picture the group presented.

"It might be better if we kept a more military appearance," suggested Lindsay, eyeing John's rumpled clothing. The young officer had barely said a dozen words to John in the days they had been out.

"That might be true if I was a soldier, but I am not," said John lightly.

"Yes. Quite. What is it you are doing here?" asked Lindsay. They were in the canoes once again and had ended up sitting side by side. They both paddled, measuring the words to the steady pattern of their strokes.

"I draw." John could not wait to hear Lindsay's reaction. "Maps, portraits of the people here." He glanced at Lindsay, whose eyes suddenly held a grudging interest.

"Portraits is it? Then you must draw me!"

That night, after their evening meal, John did. They sat by the river's edge near the fire. The remains of dinner were cleared away. Wallace and Natka sprawled in the cool sand in contented relaxation. Men smoked and coughed and talked of tomorrow. The soldiers had a fire going a small distance away. The Senecas' shaved heads were lit by the flickering of their own fire. Now and then laughter pierced the night as someone remembered a joke. Lindsay sat before John, coat buttoned, tricorne properly set on his white, wigged head. He was the perfect picture of an English officer. From where he sat on the other side of the fire, Lord MacNeil watched as John prepared to sketch.

"I will not do this for nothing," said John. "There is a price." He was readying his materials and waited to see what Lindsay might say. Wallace chuckled softly.

"A price? That is no matter. Name your price." He was a wealthy young man, the son of a Scottish Earl.

"My price is that you answer a question." John was already sketching.

Wallace laughed out loud. "Now he has you."

Lindsay ignored the guide as he ignored most people. He knew the sort well. Poor, landless, far from his wretched home in the highlands, Wallace was now as Canadian as the inhabitants. Lindsay settled himself with confidence. He was an officer in His Majesty's service. He had not come to this country to mix with the locals, but to defend the interests of the Crown.

"That seems cheap enough. Ask away, then."

John drew the young officer's face. Slender sunburned nose, strong chin, deadly serious pale-blue eyes. A straight back and steady shoulders. John paused for a moment, and the soft rasping of charcoal against paper ceased. Lindsay looked at him.

"What is it you like about this place?" asked John. Lindsay lifted his chin just a bit and gazed at him.

Careful, John, thought Lord MacNeil, though he said nothing. You may not like Lindsay, but in this place you need not purposely make enemies.

"Whatever might you mean?" asked Lindsay.

"This is my price, my question. What keeps you here? The people? The land? To me it is all a wonder." John began to sketch again. Lindsay snorted.

"I am here in service of the Crown. That is all. When all of this is over and Canada is safely British, for it is not yet you must know, then I shall be posted elsewhere, I suppose." John added the mole alongside Lindsay's mouth.

"And what of the people who live here?" asked John. "Is this not their land as well?" Wallace listened to all of this with a growing sense of unease. He was more than conscious of Natka, who sat in silence beside him. It was not an easy thing to hear your home spoken of as belonging to a conquering nation. Wallace knew Lindsay's sort. Gentry with more land than anyone could cross in a week. A house big enough for fifty crofters' families to be at home.

"This is English soil," Lindsay went on. "At least it shall be when the people are broken."

"And how will they be broken?" asked Natka. He showed no anger, only a calmness born from years of watching first one army of newcomers, then another, claim his land. Lindsay, not being entirely foolish, said no more. In time they would all know, he thought to himself.

"We be near, Captain MacNeil," said Wallace, breaking the uncomfortable silence. "Tomorrow we will reach the mouth of the Niagara and Lake Erie. The *Swift* will be there waiting. She is my boat. I expect the old lass wintered well in the hands of my wee lads."

"My son and I shall sail with you then," said MacNeil. "The canoes shall follow us. They will join us in Detroit later. Your vessel will get us there more quickly, I trust?"

Wallace nodded his answer.

"They know we are coming, your wee sons?" asked John as he drew. In a world where few roads existed and letters traveled so very slowly, it was hard to imagine getting important news anywhere quickly. "They have been waiting?"

Wallace tossed a small stick into the fire just for the pleasure of seeing it burst into flames and then said, "For a month, I would ken. News ill or fair travels quickly here, John. Letters may trail behind us, but word of mouth is like a wildfire in the wilderness."

"I have not sailed on this boat for a long while," mused Natka. "It will be interesting."

Wallace roared with laughter, although no one but Natka and John understood why.

They have all sorts of odd jokes between them, like Jane and I do, thought John, and he felt a pang of longing for his sister. John forced her and home from his mind. He packed away his paper and charcoal, telling Lindsay that they would finish up the next evening. The lieutenant nodded and, bidding John good night, went to his tent.

John lay sprawled on his back in the sand watching the stars in the clear sky. A year ago the haughty looks from a young officer such as Lindsay would have left John stuttering; now he only wondered at how out of place the lieutenant seemed. He himself felt more at ease here than he had in any other place, although he was not certain why. A bat flew by and then another. Wallace was still chuckling softly when John rolled himself in his blanket and slept.

◇ ◇

The next day seemed as though it was a journey of hundreds of miles. John could barely wait to see the *Swift* about which he had heard so much. The British had no ships on this lake yet, and warships were needed. Locked in by land and held prisoner by Niagara Falls and the rapids far to the north, they would still be able to wander as far as Lake Superior and down to the Niagara River once a navy floated on these waters.

By afternoon the river had widened and in the distance its mouth could be seen. They paddled hard, staying near the shore where the current was less strong. Finally, the canoes were steered to the beach and dragged up onto the pebbles. Beyond the trees a boat drifted at anchor.

"There she is!" cried John in excitement. The *Swift* floated on the wind-ruffled water. At one time John would have thought her tiny. Now he was struck by her size, having been so long in a canoe. At a little over forty feet, she was low and sleek. Both of her ends were pointed and a long sprit extended from her bow. A single mast of pine rose from her deck.

"We have other company," remarked Lord MacNeil who stood there in pleasant surprise. He had expected Wallace's boat to be simply another bateau. "It is a party from Detroit." MacNeil recognized Lieutenant Monroe, one of Fort Niagara's officers who had been ordered to Detroit last year. The officer was walking toward them, along with some other men.

Down the beach they had set up a camp. A large bateau was pulled up on the sand and tents had been pitched. As MacNeil watched the men approach, John went back to the canoe and rummaged in his belongings. There it was, a little rumpled, a touch disheveled. He sighed, then pulled off his hat, plunked on the wig, and placed the tricorne atop it. He walked back to where his father and their men stood.

"Did you trap something, John?" asked Wallace, stroking his beard. "Lovely wee pelt you've got on your head, lad." John tried to look cross but could not. He dared not laugh, though.

"We will trade it at the fort," mused Natka. "They will not have seen such an animal, I think."

John could not look at either of them for fear of losing control.

"Enough," rumbled Lord MacNeil, for the party of men had reached them. This was a moment of great dignity in his eyes. The officer who stood before him removed his hat and bowed; Lord MacNeil did the same.

"Welcome, Captain MacNeil, sir. And you as well, Lindsay," he said. The two lieutenants nodded to each other. Although of the same rank, Monroe seemed a very different sort of man. There was none of Lindsay's polish about him. The wilderness had left its hard marks on his face and uniform.

"Lieutenant Monroe," returned MacNeil. "We meet again. You look fit. Your men, did they winter well?"

"That they did, sir, as did all at Detroit. It was a mild winter here — well, as mild as winter in Canada ever gets, and we were comfortable enough."

Mild, thought John. What would he call cold!

"News from England?" asked MacNeil. "Get the canoes over to the encampment, men," he called over his shoulder to the soldiers who nodded and turned to the task.

"Indeed, sir. Dispatches from Albany and London and letters for you and your son." The lieutenant nodded a greeting to John, who nodded in return.

"Yes!" cried John. "Now we will know." And he wondered what strange things Jane would have to tell him. Would he have a new brother or sister? Had Jane brought down the monarchy? His father raised an eyebrow, but said nothing to him.

"We will see to them later," he said to Monroe. John and his father walked to the small camp with Monroe and his men. Wallace and Natka followed.

"There is one thing, sir. It has come by word of mouth and it is true."

"What is that?" asked MacNeil, watching the lieutenant's serious face.

"The King is dead, sir. Long live King George." Everyone stopped. In the silence, only the lonely call of a single gull rang overhead. Old King George had always been there, thought John. How strange to think we have a new king.

"God save the King," said Lord MacNeil quietly. He had heard the rumors, but kept them to himself. "When did it happen?"

"Last fall, in October," answered Lieutenant Monroe, as they again crunched through the sand and pebbles. John's low buckled shoes were already filling with small stones and bits of crushed shell.

"We were at Fort Niagara then," said John. How odd it was. Life passed here in Canada, and a world away things happened in England. Would there ever come a time when distance did not separate them so?

Suddenly there was a wild screaming and splashing from out on the lake where the *Swift* lay at anchor. They all turned and squinted out at the boat. A man was waving frantically. Two bobbing heads showed in the flat water.

"Someone has fallen in!" cried John. "Are they drowning?" Then he saw that the heads were attached to swimmers who were moving toward the beach.

"Nay," said Wallace fondly. "'Tis only my wee lads

coming to see their old father. The wee bairns are tender-hearted, and they have missed their father sorely."

The wee lads staggered out of the water. They were tall young men, sturdily built. Dripping kilts clung to their massive thighs; their shirts showed the heavy muscles that were hidden beneath. Water streamed from their long braids of black hair. In their joy to see their father, they nearly knocked him over.

"We've been here a month, Father!" shouted one of Wallace's sons, embracing him.

"With nothing to eat but fish, Father!" cried the other, who clasped his arms around both his brother and his father.

"Sean stayed behind on the boat, bless his wee soul, and sends his love, Father, and says come aboard," said the first wee lad. They both nodded to Natka who stayed well clear of their arms. He knew what a hug from one of the Doig lads could feel like.

"Hush, my wee sons, hush! You're a fine sight for these eyes, but I canna come just yet. We're in the midst of an adventure! We go to Detroit with yon Lord MacNeil and his fine son John and a few other grand fellas! What say you to that?"

"If there is food, Father, and we dinna mean fish, we will go anywhere!"

"There will be food, and the fort, and some lovely lassies, I wager. John MacNeil, greet my sons, Hamish and Alex. Lads, greet young John MacNeil." Carefully, so they would not crush it, they each shook his outstretched hand. What a wee lad he was.

"Mayhap we should leave at once, Father," suggested Alex anxiously, peering across the water.

"Aye," Hamish agreed, shifting from foot to foot. "We wouldna want to miss the lassies."

"Or the food," added Alex in hope of a decent meal.

"Never fear. They will be there," Wallace assured them. They all turned at the sound of a splash as Sean, the third wee lad, hurled himself into the lake. In a few minutes another warm Doig reunion took place on the beach.

They would not leave at once, no matter how many lovely lassies or delicious meals awaited at Fort Detroit, Lord MacNeil decided. A rest in camp and a fresh start in the morning would be wiser. By this time, the three canoes were floating just off the beach. The men unloaded the supplies and brought the canoes ashore, and a larger camp took shape. Later on, one of the Doig boys would return to the *Swift* to spend the night on board. On Lake Erie, to leave a vessel anchored and unattended overnight was to ask for disaster. It was not long before tents were up and fires crackled. The Senecas and several of the soldiers melted into the forest to hunt for game.

It was a noisy, happy camp that night. The worst of the journey was behind them, it seemed, and at last Fort Detroit was almost a reality. With their bellies filled with the broiled meat of rabbit, squirrel, and raccoon, everyone lay back in the sand and watched the sun set. As he promised, John finished the portrait of Lindsay. The young officer seemed quite pleased with it.

"A fine likeness," he said, admiring himself.

"Well, I shall keep it safely for you in my case," said John. "When we reach the fort you will have it." Lindsay nodded his agreement.

"The dispatches and letters are here, sir," said Monroe to Lord MacNeil. He had waited until they were fed and settled to burden the officer with work. He moved discreetly away, joining his men at their fire.

"Thank you, Mr. Monroe." Lord MacNeil picked up a dispatch and opened the oiled packet. In moments his mind seemed to be focused only on the papers that he held in his hand. John cleared his throat and his father looked up from the dispatch.

"My letter, Father?" he politely asked. Once he would not have dared to disturb Lord MacNeil as he worked. Now a growing confidence in himself gave him the heart to do so.

"Ah, yes. Of course, John," answered MacNeil in surprise and, picking up a thick, sealed envelope, handed it to his son. John ripped it open and read quickly.

"Yes!" he cried. His father looked up from the dispatch. Lindsay raised his brows at such a display.

"Well?" asked Lord MacNeil softly. He waited, his grip tight on the dispatch.

"You have a new son, Father, and I have a brother!" John was fairly jumping up and down with happiness.

"And your mother?" Lines of worry wrinkled MacNeil's forehead.

"Jane says she is very well." MacNeil relaxed. He had not permitted himself the luxury of turning first to home matters, when the demands of service were always more important. How hard and cold John must think him. But officers must be hard. It was hardness that had won this land for England.

"Good. That is very good." He slumped a little, then straightened again. Absorbed in their own thoughts, they each sat in silence. Then John rolled over. Sprawled on his belly in the sand with the pages tilted to catch the last rays of the sun, he read Jane's letter.

*My dear John,* she wrote. *How I wish I could have told you sooner. We have a brother. Many things have happened here, but that is the most important. Little James Edward William MacNeil was born September 14, 1760, in the night. What a large name for such a tiny baby! He will be many months old when you read this. We are all so very happy and even David cannot help smiling. Mama is tired, but in good health and she has written to Father.*

*Mary has become a tyrant. She took over the nursery like a lioness and it is now her kingdom. She will not let Winston enter, which greatly annoys him. He does like to sneak in anyway when she is not watching. He tries to peer over the crib and peek at the baby.* John could picture the little terrier, bright black eyes gleaming as it crept across the nursery floor. Like Jane, it knew just where to step to avoid the creaking floorboards.

*You surely must know that old King George has died, and that his grandson King George now rules England. His coronation will be next year. That will be this year to you. This is most confusing. His Majesty is to be wed as well. Her name is Princess Charlotte and she is only sixteen years old. Henry says that she will make a good queen. I would not make a good queen. I talk too much and cannot sit still.* John wondered who had convinced her of that fact. Her friend Viscount Henry Fitzwalter, perhaps?

*Yes, Henry says it is so,* she went on and John laughed aloud. She had read his thoughts from an ocean and a year away. So it was with twins, he supposed. *But he talks ceaselessly and wiggles as much as I do, so he should know.*

*We have been to London again. This time I took some of your drawings. Mama was there, of course. A young lady must have her chaperone, although I think it is most unfair. Do you have a chaperone? Oh, to be able to wander where I wished, dressed as I wished, doing precisely what I wished. What a grand thing that would be.*

*I learned later that Henry showed your pictures to King George. His Majesty loved your work, John. The drawings you sent to me are so different than those that came with the royal maps and dispatches. He wishes to have more so that he may see the people and the country as they truly are!*

Across the fire John's father muttered, "What has the child done now?" John looked up from his letter. He thought for a moment that his father was speaking to him, that he wanted to hear what Jane had written. Mama's letter now lay open on the sand and he saw that his father was reading another of the dispatches. Lord MacNeil gazed across at his son with a rather stunned look on his face.

"Who has done what, sir?" asked John. He began to worry.

"Jane, of course," answered his father shortly. "This is a letter from Prince George, who is now King George, our sovereign. It regards you."

"Me, sir?" said John. He sat up. Jane! You will meddle!

"It seems he has seen your drawings. At tea, for heaven's sake, with our Jane and one Viscount Henry Fitzwalter. Do I have this right or is Jane now running the palace and serving tea to everyone?"

"Yes, Henry. Jane's friend," said John faintly.

"Jane's friend. Of course! Naturally! And yours as well? No, do not tell me. I prefer to live in ignorance. Well, he has seen your drawings and wants more. Maps are no longer the issue, it appears. Since His Majesty cannot come to Canada, we are to send Canada to him." He looked up at his son. "You now have a direct line to the Crown, John. Dispatches will be sent straight from you to the King."

"Is this good or bad?" asked John hesitantly. He had thought that he had at least some measure of his father's approval these days.

"It is good news, John. I shall have to find another cartographer in time. New maps must be drawn, but that is nothing. No, it seems your heart's desire may have been granted." He shook his head in wonder. "Unofficially, you are now the King's own artist in Canada."

# CHAPTER
## S I X

John did not sleep well. All night he could think of nothing but the news from England. The King's own artist. He was not certain what it would mean, but at this moment as he lay in the cool sand of Lake Erie's beach, it sounded wonderful.

He had just shut his eyes, his mind and thoughts settled at last, when he felt the camp stirring around him. Bleary but excited, he sat up. The men were loading supplies and gear into the canoes at the water's edge. There would be a quick, cold breakfast before they departed, he supposed. John saw that his father's eyes were as red as he knew his own must be. Perhaps he had not slept much either. What had kept him awake? The news from home? The prospects of Detroit? John could not guess. As he sorted out his clothing, clapping his wig back onto his head and emptying stones from his shoes, he looked up to see Jeffrey Lindsay striding across the damp beach.

"I say, John."

John looked up in surprise. His Christian name, was

it? "Yes, Jeffrey?" he answered as he put on his shoes.

"You will be sending drawings to His Majesty the King, I hear."

"It seems I shall," said John as he stood and dusted sand from himself.

"May I make a suggestion?" Lindsay was looking off across the lake as he spoke.

"I welcome them!" How Jane would be enjoying this. She would have made short work of Lindsay weeks ago. But for all his arrogance and coldness, there was still something John must admire in the young officer. He had his nerve if nothing else.

"Excellent!" Lindsay eyed John with a slightly different attitude. How irritating that the boy and not himself had come to the King's attention. Well, perhaps that might be changed. "Then I suggest, no, I insist that you send on my portrait to His Majesty."

"A fine idea, Jeffrey!" exclaimed John. Lindsay nodded and strode away, perfectly neat, perfectly coifed, and perfectly pleased with his success. His Majesty would see that his officers had standards, Lindsay thought, walking down the beach. John smiled to himself as he watched Lindsay go.

At last they were ready. Laughter echoed over the breezy water, and sunlight sparkled on the wavelets that had begun to dance along the lake's surface. It seemed they would have a good wind to carry them along.

"We shall likely outdistance you, Mr. Monroe. Besides, you will make camp at night while we sail steadily on," said Lord MacNeil to the lieutenant. "Fare thee well, Monroe."

"Fare thee well, sir," answered Monroe. Lord MacNeil turned to Lieutenant Lindsay who stood there poised and waiting.

"And you, Mr. Lindsay, will see to it that the canoes stay with Mr. Monroe's bateau. There is strength in numbers."

"Indeed, sir," answered Lindsay, who hardly cared to remain with the soldiers and Natives. This rabble from Detroit looked worse than what they had left behind at Fort Niagara. Still, orders must be obeyed. "We shall rendezvous at Detroit, then, Captain MacNeil, sir!" Lindsay crunched off to where the bateau and canoes waited.

In a few hard heaves the bateau was floating. Monroe and his soldiers climbed in. Two men who still grasped the bateau's thwarts gave the vessel a hard shove and leaped in as it floated out onto the lake. The men rowed steadily and the bateau drew away from the shore. The canoes were already in the water, launched by their party; John and the others climbed in and they paddled to Wallace's boat.

The *Swift* was a low vessel. Her sides rode only three feet above the water's surface. They climbed up, Lord MacNeil and then John. Wallace and Natka followed them. Wallace's sons, who had been taken aboard by canoe earlier to join their brother, beamed proudly at them and slapped John's shoulders in welcome.

"We will sail at once, Mr. Doig, if you please," ordered Lord MacNeil.

"As skipper of this vessel, it does, sir," answered Wallace, clearly stating who would be in charge on the *Swift*. Lord MacNeil did not falter, nor did he take offense. It may not be a Royal Navy vessel, but a ship was a ship and its captain called the tune to which they all danced.

"Bring some of the supplies on board, if you will, then."

"Aye. Move to it, Sean and Alex."

The lads fell to the job of readying the *Swift* while everyone looked about. There was a shallow deck and a small cuddy cabin forward where supplies and sail were stored. The *Swift* had been built for speed rather than comfort. John shielded his eyes against the brightening sun and looked up at the mast. It was a single spar of pine that gleamed in the sunlight where it rose from the deck. Sturdy rope rigging held it in place.

"How in the world did you build such a boat?" he asked Wallace incredulously. His sons had brought out the carefully bundled jib and had carried it forward. A mainsail already lay on the deck, weighted down by its boom and gaff.

"An act of pure love, lad," he answered. "Years it took to cut the boards and lay the keel, to find a pine straight and true for the mast, and the spars for the gaff rig on the main."

"Dinna forget the sails, Father," reminded Sean, who was tying a rope halyard to the top of the jib.

"And all the furs it took to buy rope, canvas, and needle and thread," added Alex, who could remember long winters spent in the north tending traps and curing pelts.

"The stones for the ballast to weigh the hull down in the water, that were no mere task," Hamish said. "And the anchor? That meant many months of trapping." To John it looked as though any of Wallace's sons could have carried the entire ballast single-handedly and not broken a sweat.

Wallace had not given an order and yet the boat was now almost underway. He stood with one hand resting lightly on the tiller. The *Swift* had pointed itself into the wind as all boats at anchor will do. When Hamish pulled up the anchor, Alex raised the mainsail and Sean hoisted the jib. Wallace let the boat fall off the wind just a little and the sails began to draw. Natka braced his moccasined feet on the deck as the sloop began to pick up speed in the breeze that had risen from the southeast.

"Bring in those sails, lads," said Wallace and his sons fell to the task.

"We shall see why she is called the *Swift*," said John's father. As the sails were hauled in, she heeled over a little more. Foam began to spill out from each side of her bow. The bateau and canoes were left behind and quickly grew smaller.

"We go like the wind," said Natka. This was like flying. Still, he did not have the sense of being one with this boat as he did with a canoe.

"Father says that they will build schooners back near Fort Niagara. They are good for these waters," John told Natka. He leaned against the mast and looked out into the distance. "They are quick and you do not need so large a crew to sail them. A sloop like this is much the same." The breeze felt cool on John's face and sweaty neck. He was happy to once again be on the water with a fine boat under his feet.

"Well, 'tis a good thing it doesna need so many sailors," said Wallace as he steered. The wind lifted his kilt now and then. John hoped it did not flip the thing over his head. "We shall all be verra cozy here." They would share the open deck space for sleeping. John knew that watches would be stood and all, including him, would take their turns.

"I shall do my share," said John cheerfully. "We will be in the fort soon enough and this is grand!" He leaned out a way to look over the side and the wind caught his wig. He clamped both hands down on his head.

"It is alive, I think," observed Natka and they all laughed. It was a fine day. The sky was clear and warm, the sun shone brightly and the wind blew smartly. They were on their way and the journey was nearly over.

# CHAPTER
# SEVEN

All that summer John drew the world that was part of Fort Detroit. Sometimes he traveled by canoe with Natka and Wallace. Now and again the wee lads came along. They were often gone for days, taking some food, blankets, and John's ever-present document case.

"We do not need much," Natka said. "Bear grease to keep off insects is a good thing."

"Powder and balls and shot for the muskets," said Wallace, eyeing John carefully. "And tobacco for our pipes. But you canna voyage like that, lad, in stockings and buckled shoes. We shall fit you out so that none would ken you hadna spent years in the bush."

Lord MacNeil sighed when he saw his son ready to depart for the first time on an expedition. He said nothing though, for in truth it was sensible.

As some sort of gesture, John still wore the wig or at least carried it around. But he now had a simple long shirt, belted at the waist, rough cloth breeches, and moccasins. He carried no musket, but his case, a large leather pouch, and a wooden canteen were slung over his shoulder. A knife in a simple sheath hung from his belt. Lord MacNeil could only imagine what his wife, Lady Emma, would have thought.

Wallace and Natka chose the destinations. They went up and down the river exploring the shoreline, camping on the islands that lay downstream. John sketched herons, teals, and an endless assortment of noisy gulls; he drew the land itself and the soft clouds that drifted across the blue sky. It was a quiet break from life at the fort.

He was never left alone. This order, he suspected, had come from his father. Natka or Wallace would sit some distance off, seeming to sleep, but watching and listening for the unseen dangers that could creep up quietly. Not all men were friendly and Canada had its share of brigands with thievery or worse on their minds. While John was drawing, either Natka or Wallace hunted or fished for their evening meal. There were plump rabbits and groundhogs in the long grass and squirrels in every tree. Mallards, wood ducks, canvasbacks, and wild turkeys were there to be taken. All manner of fish, from perch and pickerel to tiny gleaming minnows, swam in the clear water.

John had sent many letters and drawings to Jane and to the King. Dispatches left nearly each week, carried by Natives or soldiers. But still, all news that reached England was old news. And all word that came back across the ocean was of things that had happened months ago. Men heard of children that had been born and knew that as they read the letters the child might be taking its first steps. But more than distance separated England from its wild possession. Canada was a world apart in its customs and the ways of the people.

Because of the fine summer weather and the good speed at which ships could cross the Atlantic, John shortly received another letter from Jane. Her writing was a sweet echo of her own dear voice.

> *The baby grows so quickly, John. I had no idea this would happen. He waves his little plump arms and makes the strangest sounds. Sometimes when Mary dozes, Winston and I sneak little Jamie out of the nursery and take him down the hall to your room. He is here now with me as I write. I do believe he is sending out his thoughts as I am. His thoughts will be mostly of milk and nappies, I suppose. Mine are of the wonderful scenes your pictures and letters show me. It is almost as though I am there. I may never see Canada, but perhaps Jamie shall when he is grown.*
>
> *I have shocking news, John, so it would be best if you are sitting. Perhaps you should lie down instead. Mama will have written Father of it. Do not tell him. She will be able to break this to him more easily.*
>
> *I am fourteen years old now, as you are. Can you recall before you left, I said I would not marry until I found someone exactly like me? You must know that I have done exactly that, and I am certain you can guess who it is.*

John had sat in wonder, unable to read any further. "If it is the King I shall faint," he said aloud in a weak voice. He braced himself and read on.

> *Undoubtedly you will be silly and think it is King*
> *George, but if you do you will be wrong. It is Henry, of*
> *course. All is quite informal at this point. Father must*
> *give his consent and there will be a long engagement.*
> *Mama does not wish me to wed until my sixteenth year.*
> *She says I should enjoy my present state. I will be a*
> *married woman all my life once the deed is done.*

He should not have been surprised. From her description of Henry and tales of their antics together, John thought he must have known in his heart all along that this young man would be perfect for his sister. How could she not marry someone on whom she had spilled punch? It was so like her. John knew that his father could not object, and he hoped that Jane and Henry would be happy. Would he ever meet someone just like himself, someone with whom he might share everything? At the moment he could not let it concern him. His days were filled with work and the pictures he drew.

When not out in the field, John wandered the fort, watching people who had business there. It was easy to see that Detroit was an important post. Key to the trading and supplies that linked the forts together, it was well defended. Cannons and mortars were kept in good working order by the soldiers who served under the fort's commander, Captain Campbell. They had to be. There had been a council here last month. Hundreds of Native warriors and their chiefs had filled the fort, voicing complaints and threatening war. But Captain Campbell, through his interpreter Pierre LaButte, had persuaded the Iroquois that peace was the best course. Other tribes had not agreed, but for the moment an uneasy truce prevailed and the military could somewhat relax.

But the military was only part of life at Detroit. An entire French community had remained behind after the French had surrendered. Blacksmiths, harness makers, and gunsmiths all worked within the fort. There were homesteads and farms up and down the river on each side of the fort and on the other side of the water. Detroit did have its own gardens just outside the walls, but often locals came to sell or trade their own produce. These French farmers grew wheat, corn, and oats. Sweet yellow pears and softly fuzzed peaches hung from their trees. They raised plump pigs and oxen, cows and tasty chickens. The soldiers were always happy for some sausage from the smokehouse of a farm wife or a haunch of venison from a deer shot by an enterprising young man.

> *If you walk through the fort you will not hear just French and English spoken*, John wrote to his sister. *The local settlers speak a dialect of their own*, patois, *Father calls it. There are hundreds of Natives around the fort. The Odawa, Miami, Potawatomi, Fox, and Sauk each speak their own tongue. Some words are the same, but not all. We get by with hand signs and the help of our translators*.

Of all the things John drew, people were his favorite. Local men and women walked Fort Detroit's neatly laid-out streets. Rue St. Joseph, Rue St. Jacques, Rue Ste. Anne, and Rue St. Louis all ran parallel to the river, while other streets crossed them north to south. Soldiers in their red coats, armed and ready with their muskets, stood on guard, watching at the walls or in one of the block houses standing at each corner.

Huge freight canoes stopped near what was called the water gate at the river. They were paddled by traders, powerfully built men dressed in trade cloth shirts and leather or cloth leggings and sturdy moccasins. Woven belts in colorful patterns circled their waists. Silk scarves were wrapped around their heads no matter what the weather. It was as much a uniform as the red coats of the British soldiers. To John's eyes, they looked more at home.

They were French, the traders. Some spoke English and many spoke the dialects of the tribes with whom they traded or the women they married. They carried in bales of beaver pelts. The Crown now wanted to keep a tight hold on the fur trade it had won when it took Canada from France. That meant that all trading was done inside the fort, and an endless stream of all sorts of people came and went.

Word soon spread that the son of a newly arrived officer was there among them and that he drew pictures. "*Dessinez-moi!*" the trappers called when they saw John, "Draw me!" And they argued among themselves for the honor.

"Be gone, Armand, you ugly piece of beaver dirt! A face like a prune you have."

"En you, Etienne? Dat visage of yours, she would scare a person away. It scare me!"

John drew them all.

The *Swift* sailed out often. Lord MacNeil called it making the King's presence felt. He believed that patrolling up the river and into Lake St. Clair had a reassuring effect on the locals. Somehow he had persuaded Wallace to fly the British colors. The sight of the sloop scudding along under full sail reminded people that these were now English waters. John did not know or care. He simply enjoyed setting out on the *Swift* each time his father planned an expedition, particularly one into Lake St. Clair.

John studied the maps and charts in his father's quarters at the fort many times. Lake St. Clair was a shallow lake. Even though Wallace's boat drew little water and could float in only a few feet, they had to take soundings when they went into any unfamiliar area. On the charts it looked small, but in the light summer winds, Lake St. Clair took many hours to cross.

One morning at the very end of August, the *Swift* set out. They were a small party — John, his father, Wallace, and Natka. Six soldiers accompanied them, but the three wee lads had elected to stay behind. There was an active social life at the fort; Wallace's wee lads felt quite at home it seemed. The commander, Captain Campbell, held dances and gatherings each Sunday evening that usually lasted into the early morning hours. Wallace's sons had all struck up friendships with French girls, and spending time with the lovely, young women had cut sharply into their sailing.

John stood at the bow, breathing in the fine, morning air. A slight mist hung over the river, but it was quickly lifting in the sunshine and rising breezes. Both sails were flying. The boat held its own as it sailed up the river against the powerful current. John watched as they passed a small island at the river's mouth. For some reason, he had not yet explored it with Natka and Wallace.

"We will sail as far as the end of the lake and the next river," announced Lord MacNeil, who could not help commanding, "then back again." Wallace nodded. It was his plan as well.

The *Swift* sailed all day. A clear, hot sky curved over them and the air warmed quickly. Near the far end of the lake, the ship tacked, swinging slowly about in the light breeze and headed back across the water. The wind grew lighter still and the sails began to draw less. Finally, by late afternoon they were just ghosting, almost drifting in the nearly still air. Clouds of gnats swarmed here and there; men wiped sweat from their faces. It was damp and close. The scent of water and the boat's hot decks filled John's nose. They were just east of the small island that lay near the mouth of the Detroit River. Pêche Island, it was called.

"We will anchor here," said Lord MacNeil. "If the wind comes up, we will sail back to the fort. If not, we will spend the night." They had done this sort of thing before. The *Swift* had oars, but it was a long haul back to the fort. They had water and provisions and on such a warm day as this, with the steamy night that would follow, it would be pleasant to sleep out under the stars.

Wallace directed the dropping of the sails and preparations to anchor. Soon the *Swift* lay stopped in the lake, straining against her anchor line, pulled by the ceaseless current of the river.

"Excuse me, sir," said one of the soldiers.

"Yes, Corporal," answered MacNeil.

"The men, sir. They have asked, might they swim?"

"I see no reason why they cannot," answered MacNeil. "Just make certain part of the watch is on board at all times."

"Aye, sir!" Men scattered. They began to strip, some right to their skin, others down to their britches. They hurled themselves into the water or dove off the ship gracefully. Droplets splashed on the hot deck and the smell of wet wood rose in the afternoon air.

John opened his document case and pulled out a sheaf of papers. That morning he had begun to draw Natka. The picture was almost finished, and he turned to his work again. Natka was a good model — he had a stillness about him that made sitting easy for him to do.

In one of his endlessly growing letters to Jane he had written, *The man does not talk much. I do believe that he seems to feel that words are important and should not be wasted. His mouth, as you see, is a thin stroke in a well-lined face. I think Natka is not an old man. It is that this country simply leaves its marks on people.*

Natka's red-brown skin was made more red by the sunburn from which they all suffered. His tattooed arms and torso were speckled with insect bites. Clouds of mosquitoes and midges made sitting ashore difficult unless wood smoke drifted in the air. He wore only a breech cloth and a belt hung with his weapons in this damp heat. Still, small beads of sweat pocked his face and trickled down his forehead. Sunlight washed across him and lit the odd planes and angles of his body.

They heard splashing. Wallace heaved himself up on deck. Water streamed from his long hair and beard.

"Keep an eye on yon cloud, lad. It may do something," he said and John turned to look. A small haze of fluffy white rested low in the sky to the east. What could such an innocent cloud do?

"Is it a storm? The sky is blue and it is a fine day," said John, wiping his hands on his shirt. He must always watch some cloud or the waving of the grass or the movement of the water. He leaned over the side of the ship and looked down at the lake below. Its cool promise turned his mind from his drawing.

"It is too warm, Natka. Why will you not say that it is too warm?" Natka did not complain. There was no point to it, he had told John once.

"It is too warm," said Natka and a white smile split his dark face. "Come. Let us swim."

Natka slipped off his moccasins and dropped his belt and weapons to the deck. He had no fear that anyone would touch them. He dove from the ship into the deep water, raising scarcely a ripple. John shielded his eyes with his hand. The air was still; only that haze hung to the east. He tore off his damp wig and dropped it on the deck next to his document case. John's wig generally lay in a wilted pile somewhere or another these days. He had once seen Natka poke at it with the toe of a moccasined foot, shaking his head. Then John kicked off his moccasins and pulled his shirt over his head.

Natka watched from the water. "Too many clothes," he called to John.

John tried to picture himself dressed as Natka did in this weather. "Yes, well, a breech cloth is not the regulation dress of the British military," he yelled and he leaped in, arms and legs flailing wildly. Cool water closed over his head. He came up sputtering.

"That is sad," said Natka. "You dive like a shot goose coming out of the sky." He directed John back up onto the deck and climbing up after him, tried to teach him to dive.

"You think about it too much, lad," laughed Wallace, who watched them. He was now again clad decently in his kilt. "In fact, you think too much about almost everything."

Finally, John simply swam for a while, staying close to the side of the *Swift*. Natka surfaced near John, spouting water.

"That is enough swimming for now," he said.

"I think I will stay in just a while longer," John answered. Natka grabbed the boat's rail and heaved himself up.

"Out," he said and pointed to the sky. Gray, hazy clouds were gathering and a slight breeze ruffled the surface of the lake. A harder puff of wind set the boat to swinging slightly against its mooring. John snatched at the rail and began to pull himself up. Natka offered a hand to help. John felt something changing in the air; he could almost smell it. The hairs on his arms rose. He pushed his dripping hair from his face. Looking over at Natka, he saw that the Odawa was staring at the sky.

"I do believe we are about to get some weather," Lord MacNeil observed tensely. Small ripples shivered along the warm water and then grew into wavelets with amazing speed. The last men swimming in the lake paddled to the ship. John watched the suddenly darkened sky as he quickly pulled on his shirt and struggled into his moccasins.

"Weigh the anchor, lads," called Wallace. "Prepare to set sail." The soldiers moved quickly. The *Swift* had begun to pull even harder against her anchor, and the wind now drove her as well as the current. Strong gusts built to a steady, hard wind. The color of the sky went to a strange, greenish-yellow. Men struggled to ready the boat to sail.

Then in the distance, a small twist of slate-gray cloud began to pull out from the sky. Slowly it grew and snaked lower. With an awful sound it touched the earth. John could see bushes and trees being sucked into the funnel as it widened.

"What is it?" he screamed to Natka.

"A terrible wind that will take you into the sky, John!" shouted Natka. "Lie flat on the deck or tie yourself on!"

Men strained at the line as they slowly drew back the anchor up onto the boat. At the same time, the mainsail was hoisted. The canvas flapped and cracked. At that moment, the wind roared and the air went white with spray as well as with leaves and grit from the shore. The *Swift* leaned over hard and Wallace held the tiller with all his strength, trying to turn her away from the wind.

John scrambled to catch his document case, which was now rolling across the deck. He flipped its strap over his head and secured it across his shoulder. The cap was on tight; not even rain would wet what was inside it, he knew. His wig, that hated object of discomfort, went cartwheeling past him and sailed off the deck into the water. Without a thought, John jumped for it and in that moment, the ship went one way and he went the other. His body arched gracefully in a perfect dive. In the wild confusion and blinding rain no one saw.

The *Swift* began to move, not with the stately pace with which it usually went into motion, but with a trembling and groaning that could be felt by everyone. As the real force of the storm hit the canvas, she gave a sharp heel to starboard. When John popped to the surface, the *Swift* was hard under sail, racing down toward the river with the wind behind her.

John screamed for help, but the storm screamed louder. Even if they had heard him, it would have been impossible to turn Wallace's boat, so powerful were the forces that dragged her from him. All he could do was struggle to keep his head above the water. As he gasped for breath, he saw Jane in his mind's eye and wondered what she would have thought of such a storm.

# CHAPTER
# EIGHT

On the island, Marie felt the storm coming long before it screamed down the lake. All day as she fished, baiting her hook with bits of crayfish, her eyes had gone again and again to the sky. It was unpredictable, this lake. You do not like the weather? Wait a few minutes and it will change, they said. She had learned from the time she was a small child not to take the lake and the weather for granted. You may be swimming under a clear summer sky, but that did not mean it would not open and soak you to the skin when you least suspected it. The winter ice may look thick enough to walk upon, but the water was very cold when you fell through.

"Don't go too far, Samuel," she called to her brother. Marie had stopped fishing some time ago. They had enough perch now for a feast. Her catch lay gutted and wrapped in fresh leaves at their camp. It hung from a tree in a woven, willow basket so that thieving raccoons would not get it with their clever hands.

Marie watched Samuel as he picked his way down the beach. Their dog, a large gray creature with a curling

tail, trotted along behind him. Now and again Dog —
for that was the clever name her brother had given the
animal — stopped to sniff and lift his leg. Samuel always
roamed around, led by one thing or another. An unusual
bird, the sound of frogs in the shallows, a dot of bright
color on the sand or in the grass was enough to turn his
thoughts away from whatever it was he should be doing.
Samuel was a wanderer. His life might take him to exciting places in time; she could already see the path hers
would offer. Even last summer her mother had tried
to keep her from the island and the carefree existence
it offered.

"She is a woman now of fourteen, Pierre," her mother
complained, "and she should act like a woman. She will
marry soon. She should be married now!" Marguerite
Ouabankikove shook her head and her braid swung
across her back. The braid was still mostly black and, in
spite of the years, her cheeks were smooth and soft.

Amongst the Miami, her own people, Marguerite's life
would have been very different. It seemed to Marie that
life in her mother's village was hard on everyone, but
on a woman it was the hardest. The work in the fields,
making a home with other families in the longhouse, the
trek to the winter hunt camps far to the north and west
each year were an endless circle. Oh, there was still much
work in her own life. Marie helped her mother with
everything, but their home was in one place. The cabin
that Père had built on the river a league or so from Fort
Detroit was well chinked with moss and clay against the
cold winter winds. Some day when she herself married,

Marie knew she would have a home just like it.

"Let her be, Mère," Pierre said. "She will marry soon enough, next year I will say. If that happens, then this will be the last summer she is a girl. Let her be a girl for a while longer. She will be a woman for the rest of her days."

And the matter ended there, more or less. Marie would have one more summer to run about with her legs scratched and her nose burned red, fishing and paddling up to Pêche Island. She and Samuel had a camp of sorts, a sturdy shelter from the rain, with some pots and blankets and changes of clothing for the nights they stayed over. This was to be the last summer for such things.

"And she talks too much. They both talk too much," Margeurite tossed back, her cheeks flushed with the arguing. She would have the last word.

"Now which one of us could they have got that from, I ask myself?" Pierre wondered affectionately.

Just before the storm rose, Marie and Samuel had walked up the beach. Moist air, fragrant with the scents of the woods and lake, made her heavy braid weigh damply against her neck. Her long cloth blouse hung loosely on her, but still she was hot. Marie waded into the river and, stooping, splashed water on her face. She pulled her skirt up high over her knees and tucked its hem into her belt. Stepping carefully to avoid the sharp-edged clams that lay open in the rippled sand, she tried to cool herself. Even just this far into the water she could feel the powerful current of the Detroit River.

It sucked against her brown legs, making small eddies around them.

She waded back to the beach and sat in the hot sand with her feet and legs in the water. Wavelets lapped around her ankles. Marie watched the sailing boat that was anchored out on the water. Men swam around it. They looked like small white specks dropping from the deck as they dove. Tiny shapes moved through the water. She knew they couldn't see her here on the beach since she was too far away. But even at this distance, the sound of their splashing and laughter carried across the water to her. Samuel and Dog had returned. Her brother skipped stones and chattered in the half-French, half-Miami mixture they spoke at home. Wearing only a breech cloth and silver earrings in this heat, his small body looked sleek and cool.

"Let us swim out to that bateau, Marie," Samuel suggested. His sister sighed. He did say odd things. Dog padded over and settled next to her in the sand. Marie scratched his gray ears.

"You know we cannot swim that far, Samuel. Besides, what would we do when we got there?" She complained, but she loved to hear her brother make up stories. Their father had always told them tales and Samuel was even better at it than him. Give the boy an idea and he would create something, although often the stories got jumbled together.

"Well, we will take the English back to the fort at Detroit. They like it there. Then we will sail the bateau across the ocean to France. Maybe England." He skipped another stone and smiled his gap-toothed smile at her. At seven years of age, he had lost all of his front teeth that summer. "I will be the chief of the ship and you will be the warrior."

"One warrior?" teased Marie with exaggerated surprise. "It is not much of a war party with one warrior." She leaned back on her elbows, squinting up at her brother.

"Dog will be the second warrior. Besides, it is not a war party. We come in peace," he explained patiently, splashing through the water as he talked.

"Well, it is not much of a party of any sort. Besides, I want to be the chief," she argued mischievously, suspecting what her brother would say.

"Well, you cannot, you know." He shook his head so that the black, shoulder-length hair swung freely. "You are a girl."

Marie sighed. That was the problem. Samuel might see it all for himself some day. He was a boy and could sail across the water. She would never know the sort of life he could have. A small cabin, a family, watching her children grow — those events would be her life. The fishing would end; her canoe would lie in the sand and rot. She turned her thoughts away from such things. It was too fine a day.

Marie dreamed of sailing to France or England, wherever they were, far across the ocean, which her father had described many times. It had salted water in it. How odd. She had been to the fort many times with her father, even before the English had come and the French soldiers had left. She knew how the people lived in their big houses. Through the windows she had seen elegant ladies and uniformed men sipping tea or dancing in the evenings, but what was it like in England and France? Could they be so very different from this place?

Marie listened to the island's quiet. "Don't go too far," she called over her shoulder to Samuel, who was already wandering away, making up some new game for himself and Dog. She suddenly realized that it was too quiet, that all the birds had stopped singing and that even the endless hum of cicadas and early crickets was gone. She stood and scanned the sky. Water dripped down her legs and from the hem of her skirt. Then she heard something. It began with a sudden rush of wind in the trees. Leaves turned backward and small branches began to break and fly madly through the air.

"Samuel!" she called and her brother came leaping from the woods. Dog raced alongside him, ears flattened against his head.

"Look at the sky, Marie!" he cried as he ran. "Look at the sky!"

There, across the river to the south, deep purple clouds arched over the trees. Lightning forked in silvery tongues and thunder rumbled. The wind began to blow harder and from the clouds, a long spout of gray slowly descended. Marie grabbed her brother's arm.

"We must get off the beach!" she screamed, and she could barely hear herself above the wind and crackling lightning. She pulled Samuel into the trees and dragged him down into a hollow. Dog squeezed in beside them. Marie could feel the animal trembling.

The funnel of cloud raced along the shoreline across the river, tearing up small trees and bushes. The sailing boat just off the east point of the island heeled sharply as the wind filled its rigging. Then, carried by the current and the violent storm, its sails bulging, it shot down the river. It disappeared into the heavy rain as whitecaps churned around it. For a few moments the tornado's tail whipped and thrashed. It left the ground and touched down again. At last it began to disappear back into the clouds, waving itself lazily. Leaves and twigs blew through the air and stuck to their sodden clothing. Rain sheeted down as Marie and Samuel hid their faces against each other, and the storm raged around them.

# CHAPTER
# NINE

John struggled to keep his head above the water. Rain drove into his eyes, and spume blew from the top of the foamy waves that rose quickly in the tremendous wind. He felt as though his clothing would drag him down, but he could not get out of his shirt or breeches.

The current pulled at his legs. There was no undertow — the lake was simply racing to the river as it always did and it carried John with it. The savage wind raised whitecaps. John coughed and choked from the heavy rain and the spray that splashed against his face and washed over his head. He still held mindlessly to the document case, which, filled with air and sealed closely, was floating in his arms. John could not see a thing. With the waves he could barely swim. He swallowed a huge mouthful of water and, coughing wildly, disappeared under the river's surface.

◇ ◇

Marie and Samuel lay curled together for a long while as the storm wore itself out. Finally, the force of the rain began to falter and then stopped. The wind fell. They lifted their heads and looked out through the bushes that rose above them. Dog scrambled to his feet and shook himself. They climbed from the hollow and walked out onto the beach. Their canoe was gone, ripped from where it had been beached on the sand away from the waves and lifted into the sky by the storm. Thunder rumbled in the distance.

"Père will come for us," said Samuel with confidence. He loved his father blindly. Marie sighed. She could only think of the damp night they would spend on the island. She hoped her parents would not worry.

Samuel, of course, wandered off with Dog to inspect the changes the storm had made to the beach. Although the funnel cloud had been nowhere near them, branches and leaves lay plastered against everything. Far down the sand just before the elbow of land that poked out into the river, some white thing lay half in and half out of the water.

"It must be a bird," said Marie as she walked toward her brother. "Some poor gull was caught in the wind and beaten down." Marie felt her heart go out to the creature. She fished and crabbed and picked clams from the shallows, but Marie could not bring herself to hunt. She had to harden herself when she skinned the game her father and brother brought home. The glazed eyes of rabbits and small deer sometimes stared at her in her dreams.

Dog reached the thing first. His hackles rose and he growled softly. Samuel squatted near the white lump and picked it up with a stick.

"It's someone's hair!" he cried. For a moment Marie felt a sick thrill of fear and disgust. She had seen men once with scalps at their belts. Then she laughed.

"It's a wig," she said to Samuel. The white powder was gummy and tangled with weed.

Samuel put it on his head laughing. He bowed to her and held out his hand.

Marie laughed and curtsied as she had seen the ladies in the fort do. At that moment they saw a figure turn the corner of the point and walk unsteadily toward them.

"Hello!" called John in a shaky voice, stunned at the fact that he was still alive and able to speak at all. He remembered his moccasins had brushed the river's bottom and then a great wave had washed him onto the beach. When he had opened his eyes, John lay on his back in the wet sand. Storm clouds still swirled above him, but the rain had nearly stopped and the awful roar of the whirlwind was gone. He sat up carefully and finally let go of the document case. His fingers and hands ached, his eyes were raw and reddened, and his stomach was unpleasantly full of water. The struggle to rise to his feet made his head spin. The document case bumped heavily against his belly. John dropped to his knees and vomited, lake water emptying out of him. He wiped his mouth on his sleeve and then on trembling legs, he stood once again.

Now Marie and Samuel stared at the bedraggled form picking its way down the beach. Dog's ears perked up, and he stood ready for whatever danger might come.

"He must be from that boat," whispered Samuel, and his sister nodded as she watched the boy come closer. She saw someone about her age. He was her height and she was not tall; a leather case was slung over his shoulder. Long, dark hair was tied back from his neck, wet tendrils sticking to his skin. He had clear, gray eyes and a skiff of freckles scattered across the bridge of his nose. There was the look about him of a young boy who had just passed childhood, who had stepped uncertainly into the world of men. He seemed very English, very serious, but then he smiled.

"I see you have found my wig," he announced and the white smile changed his face. He saw their blank expressions and then said the same words again in French. His eyes crinkled as he watched them.

"How can you be sure it's yours?" asked Samuel grumpily. He meant to defend his right to keep what he had found. Dog cautiously circled the stranger, sniffing at his legs and feet.

"Oh, it is mine. I would know that thing anywhere," John answered, brushing wet hair back from his forehead. He stared at the girl who stood across from him. She was as slim and straight as a boy, but the wet clothing that stuck to her left no doubt that beneath it was a young woman. She had a sweet, oval face and, strangely enough, green eyes. A glossy black braid hung over her shoulder. It had come undone and she was absentmindedly braiding it up again. John suddenly thought of Mary braiding his sister's wild hair each night.

"Give it to him, Samuel. It is his. Who else could own

it?" She looked directly at John. "He is just a boy. He does not know he cannot keep all that he finds. Besides, he has never seen such a thing so closely." Then she smiled at her brother's childishness, and John saw how lovely she was.

"Well, he shall have it then. I make a gift of it to you," said John to the little boy. Samuel grinned.

"The funnel, did you see it?" asked John, turning to the girl.

"Yes!" cried Samuel, answering for his sister. "It nearly sucked that bateau into itself and carried it away." He stopped at the look of alarm on John's face.

"My father and men from the fort were on that boat," he said softly and his face stiffened. "What happened? I could not see from the water." His heart was pounding hard in his chest. Until that moment he did not know how much he loved his father.

"It sailed away," answered Marie. He does not seem English, she thought suddenly, for a reason she could not understand. They never look this way. "The sails were up and it went very fast."

"Good," said John in relief as he looked down at the wet sand. "They are safe then. I am sure of it. Even a storm such as that would not be too much for Wallace Doig and James MacNeil."

"Doig?" said Marie. "The man Doig with the boat that sails swiftly?" Samuel was now dancing about, twirling his wig on the stick.

"Yes, the *Swift*. It is our boat," John answered. "Well his, but we sail with him. You know it then?"

"It is the fastest bateau on the lake!" yelled Samuel as he ran in circles. "It is faster than the swallow! Faster than the eagle!" He tripped over his own feet and fell into the wet sand. Dog barked in excitement. "It is faster than me!" John and Marie laughed at the sand stuck all over Samuel. He lay there on his back.

"He makes no sense," she said to John, shrugging her shoulders.

"I am Samuel, chief of the Miami, and you are my warriors," said Samuel sternly in his deepest voice. "Both of you, and Dog as well." Dog wagged his tail at the sound of his name and panted happily.

"I am John MacNeil, son of Lord MacNeil." And he bowed to them.

"I am Marie Roy and this is my brother who thinks he is a chief today." They laughed again. "I have heard of you, John MacNeil." Everyone had heard of this boy who made the pictures. Friends of her father, two trappers, had shown them the drawings the young man had made of them. The sketches looked exactly like the bearded, laughing Frenchmen. Thunder rumbled again and this time it sounded louder and closer. Samuel's eyes widened as he looked to his sister.

"We must go to the camp," said Marie, frowning at the clouds that were building once more. "At least we will be dry there. It may storm again."

"Not a big wind, Marie," Samuel said in Miami as he stood. For him Miami was the language of his infancy. He spoke it when he was afraid.

"No, Samuel, no. No big wind. Do not fear," she said

soothingly to the nervous boy, but her eyes went to the sky again. She took his hand and started out. Dog followed. John watched them, uncertain of what to do. He must wait for the *Swift*. Surely they would come back for him.

"It will not return for you now," said Marie, and again John thought of his sister who often seemed to know his thoughts. "You must come with us." He just stood there and she sighed. Boys! Big or little they were much the same. A fork of lightning shot out of the sky and thunder boomed. Samuel whimpered. Marie reached out and, taking John's hand, pulled him along.

He was so surprised he said nothing, only walked along at her quick pace. He had never touched a girl's hand before. His mother's, of course, and Jane's and he supposed Mary's, but this was different. All those English hands had been soft and pale, untouched by work. Marie's palm was warm and rough. Once he was walking steadily beside her, she let his hand slip away. Part of John was greatly relieved. Another part of him wished he still held that warm hand in his own.

"I should have stayed to watch for the boat," he muttered in confusion. They were well into the woods now and the beach was behind them.

"No. The boat went far down the river," said Marie, remembering the way it had flown away in the storm. "And night will come. When they return it will be in daylight."

John supposed this was true. For now there was nothing but to follow this determined girl and her brother.

# CHAPTER
## TEN

Inside the forest the sounds of the rough lake and the waves that beat upon the beach were almost gone. Wind rustled through the trees. Drops of rain showered down from the leaves. There was a path here; someone had walked this way many times, John realized. It wound through the beeches and maples, then led along a reed-edged canal in which flowing water ran. Bulrushes waved in the wind and damselflies lifted from the cattails when the brown heads wobbled back and forth. In the quiet pools, pink and yellow water lilies gleamed, their open blossoms dappled with droplets. Dog stopped to drink from the water, wading in until his belly nearly touched.

"You could paddle a canoe all through here," said John in surprise.

"We do, sometimes," explained Samuel, who seemed to be regaining his spirits now that they were away from the beach and his fright from the storm. "The canals run all through the woods. But we cannot do that today. Our canoe was taken by the storm."

"Do you live on this island?" asked John. Dog frisked around his legs, threatening to trip him up.

"No, we live not so far from the fort," answered Marie. "Pêche Island is just a good place to come."

"We escape our parents!" bragged Samuel. "Mère and Père hold us prisoner." He was leaping about again, twirling the wig on the stick. Dog growled at the unfamiliar object as though it held some threat.

"That is terrible, Samuel!" scolded Marie. What would this English boy think of them? But John only laughed.

"I escape my father when I can. Sometimes it seems as though I am a prisoner, too." Marie smiled in spite of herself. Were parents the same everywhere?

"Well, it is good to escape for a little while," she said. But in time there would be no more escape for her. She pushed the thought away. "Stop. Let us go this way for a moment." And she moved into the bushes. Samuel followed and John trailed behind. Their wet clothing was made wetter by the raindrops that spilled from the branches as they passed through.

There in a clearing hidden by vines and shrubs was an apple orchard. These were not wild apple trees, the sort that spring up from seeds sown by birds or a carelessly tossed core. Someone had cleared away the brush and planted these trees in neat rows. They were pruned and clipped and their branches hung with fruit. Most of the apples were still green, but some up higher had begun to turn red where the sunlight easily reached them.

"We will pick a few," said Marie. "Only a few." And she boosted herself up onto a branch. John saw a flash of slender, brown leg and turned away, his cheeks warm. Marie threw apples to her brother. Six or seven would be enough. She jumped down and tossed one to John. He bit into the fruit and juice rushed into his mouth. Until then he had not realized he was so hungry.

"Whose place is this?" he asked as he chewed. "Someone planted these trees and cares for them."

"They are the trees of my father's friend, Pierre LaButte," Marie answered. "He has a house at the fort, but he sometimes stays in the gardener's cabin. He has planted apple trees near the gardens there as well." John nodded. He knew LaButte's cabin with its small palisade and orchard that stood outside the fort, and he had seen the man talking with his father or Captain Campbell.

"LaButte is Pontiac's interpreter," said John.

"Yes," Marie said. "He is." She was walking again, and they followed her back through the bushes and down the narrow path. The wind still blew and thunder sounded, but now it came from very far away. John looked up through the branches. Clear sky showed in a few places between the clouds. Perhaps there would not be another storm.

Then the path ended. They stood in a clearing near a narrow canal. This was the camp. John had expected something simple, but it was clear that Marie and Samuel had worked hard to make this place comfortable. A dwelling stood off from the center. It was a dome-shaped structure made of arched poles covered with hides and rush mats. Dog raced about happily, sniffing familiar smells. Marie crossed the clearing and flung back the hides that hung over the doorway.

"It is a good thing we replaced some of those mats on the wigwam this spring, Samuel," she said. She turned to John. "It leaked last fall, but all is dry inside." John looked in. There were covered baskets and pots and piles of neatly folded, striped blankets on sleeping platforms. Gourds and unhusked, dried corn hung from poles. Fresh green rushes lay on the floor.

"You did all this?" John asked in amazement.

"Yes," laughed Marie. "Who would have done it for us? It has taken a few summers to finish, but it is a fine camp now." She did not like to think that the camp was finished, especially since her summer days here were likely finished as well. Again she pushed such thoughts away and turned to something more important.

"I'm hungry!" said Samuel. "When will we eat?"

"So, you're hungry, are you?" she asked Samuel and he nodded. "And you?" She looked at John, who nodded as well. "And you, I suppose?" Dog barked and wagged his tail.

"Hungry enough to cook and eat that wig," John said and Samuel groaned at the thought.

"Well, you must both work for your meal, then. Only Dog does not. John, there is dry firewood inside the wigwam. Samuel, get the fish down out of the tree."

What did that mean? John wondered. Fish in the tree? Marie went into the shelter and picked up two clay pots. John glanced around until he saw a hide-covered pile against the wall. He pulled off the skin and filled his arms with dried tinder and branches.

"Out here," said Marie and he followed her outside to a stone-ringed firepit. He set aside the wood and placed tinder in the pit. A few steps away, Samuel was untying the rawhide rope that held a basket suspended from a tree branch. He then carried the basket to his sister who knelt before the firepit.

"Fish in a tree!" laughed John. Of course. Natka hung food from tree branches when they camped.

"Get the strike-a-light, Samuel," said Marie, and the boy ran into the wigwam and back out again with a leather pouch. He opened the pouch and pulled out a piece of flint and a curved, horn-shaped piece of steel. Samuel set cattail fluff in the pit near the dry tinder and began to strike the flint and steel. John watched him. The steel strikers and flints were common trade goods at the fort. Most men carried them in their tobacco pouches. Even John carried one when he camped out with Wallace and Natka. He had worked hard to learn how to start a fire; he could now do it. But Samuel had the sparks flying and small tendrils of smoke rising much more quickly than John could have done. The little boy fed more dry tinder to the tiny flame and then, as it snapped and caught and began to grow, he placed thin sticks on the fire.

Marie insisted that they change into dry clothing. She always made certain that extra moccasins and a few garments were there in the camp. She could do nothing about John's wet breeches, but she had some old shirts of her father's that she sometimes wore and one would fit him. They took turns changing inside the shelter. First Samuel and John peeled off their wet clothing and put on the dry things. When they emerged, Marie slipped inside the wigwam and dropped the leather flaps. Moments later, she stepped out into the clearing wearing a dry shirt and petticoat. They all hung their clothing on the bushes to dry.

"We had coals this morning," said Marie irritably as she began to prepare the food. "The storm soaked them. Cut ten green sticks, John. We will put the fish on them and grill them." She took fish from the basket as John walked to a tree and lopped off several sticks with the knife he wore at his belt. He held them up.

"Long enough?" he asked and she nodded.

"Run the sticks through the fishes' mouths and out the tails. Put two on each stick." John did as she told him. His hands were soon covered in glittering scales. When he was finished, Marie placed the fish across the basket. The three young people sat quietly on the stones that served as benches near the firepit. Dog flopped down and rested his head on his paws.

"When the flames die a bit we will grill the fish. There are wild onions in this little pot and clams in the big one. The onions we will bake in wet leaves near the small coals. There should be enough wet leaves after all this rain."

The clouds had all blown away; a hard wind was coming from the north. Overhead, swallows swooped for the day's last insects. They rose and fell, rose and fell in the air, hunting for the mosquitoes humming in the shadows.

"Did you catch all of these fish?" John asked Samuel.

"Oh, yes!" bragged the little boy. He is going to start up again, Marie sighed to herself. "I catch many fish. You know, it made me think of a story when I saw you come from the lake like that. What is it, Marie? The one about the big fish that swallowed the man?" Marie smiled innocently as she raised her shoulders in a silent no.

"It is Jonah. A whale swallowed him," offered John, poking at the fire with a stick.

"I do not know whales. I think a sturgeon swallowed you and spit you back up," said Samuel. Marie covered her mouth with her hand to hide her smiles.

"I do not know sturgeon. What is it?" asked John. He truly did not.

"Big fish, as big as me. Bigger!" cried Samuel. John looked at Marie doubtfully, but she nodded.

"You eat the eggs," she told him. This made no sense to John.

"And they have long whiskers, like a wildcat," added Samuel, and he wiggled his fingers near his face.

"Whiskers and eggs? Sounds like a strange sort of cat. But I think I have seen such a thing. Let me draw it." He slipped the leather case from off of his shoulder and pried off its lid. As he had known they would be, the papers inside were dry. He pulled them out, along with a charcoal pencil. Samuel scurried over to sit near him, and Marie leaned in closely. John began to sketch. There before their eyes, a creature appeared on the paper. It had the pointed ears, curving mouth, and whiskers of a cat, but its body was that of a fish. The whole thing ended in a long, bushy tail. Marie laughed out loud, and clapped her hands.

"Yes, that's it!" cried Samuel excitedly. John passed him the drawing.

"Keep it," he said and Samuel shivered with delight. The little boy ran to the wigwam to put it in a safe, dry place.

How kind the English boy is, Marie thought. She examined the fire. Its coals were glowing, so she stood and went to the bushes that ringed the camp. She quickly plucked handfuls of large wet leaves for the onions. The clams would bake in their own juices.

"Let me," said Samuel, who had returned to her side, and he scooped clams one by one from the pot. They had rested there since the morning, open in the cool lake water. Now, pulled by his hand from their quiet cave, they snapped shut. Samuel liked to see how quickly he could get them before they closed.

"When you put them in the pot like that, there is almost no sand in the clams," Marie told John. "They clean themselves." She dropped the clams into the coals and poked them down. The leaf-wrapped onions went in next, and then they jammed the speared fish into the sand over the pit. In short while the scent of their dinner rose into the evening air. A few late-season fireflies flickered in the shadows, and frogs began to croak.

"It smells good," said John, and Marie nodded. Samuel shifted restlessly and someone's stomach growled.

It did not take the food long to cook and they were soon nibbling crisp, grilled fish from the green sticks. With the sweet, baked onions, the clams, and yesterday's gallette, the flat bread that was baked when out in the bush, it was a delicious meal. Everyone fed Dog bits of this and that. It was comfortable, with dry clothing on their backs and warm food in their stomachs. Marie packed away the leftover food in the willow basket and again suspended it from the branch. There would be enough for breakfast.

The sun was setting and the woods were growing dark. There was a cool dampness in the air. Slowly the color of the sky deepened, changing from dark blue to black. Stars came out, and when John stood again to toss another branch onto the fire, they washed the sky with their silvery spangle. The wind blew hard from the north; they could hear it in the trees. John suspected it would blow that way all night. He sat and reached for his document case. He could not write to Jane at this moment, although his fingers itched to take up the quill and small bottle of ink he carried everywhere. Instead he pulled out charcoal and paper. He paused a moment before he spoke.

"May I draw you?" he asked Marie, and she blinked in surprise. He could see even in the firelight how her cheeks grew pink.

"Yes, draw her!" said Samuel. "And give her a long tail and whiskers." Marie shot him the special look of disdain that she reserved for her small, wild brother. She smoothed her hair and tried to straighten her blouse. John began to sketch.

"Samuel, you sound just like my sister," he said absently as the portrait took shape. "She will say anything."

"You have a sister?" said Marie curiously. "Is she young like Samuel?"

"No," answered John, carefully smudging lines he had drawn to create the suggestion of her fine cheekbones. "We are the same age. We are twins but we do not look at all alike."

"How can that be?" asked Samuel, who was tossing small wood chips into the fire.

"I do not know, but it is the truth," John replied. "See for yourself. Here." He set down the charcoal and paper and took other sheets from the case. He held one out to Marie, and Samuel crawled over to look. "I drew that on the ship as we crossed the ocean. I wanted to remember Jane just as she was when I left."

Marie saw a young girl with large, gray eyes. Straight brows sat over them and a wide mouth was curved slightly in a smile. This picture was done in terra cotta chalk and John had tinted it with soft, earth-colored washes. The girl's ash-blonde hair waved away from her forehead and, although drawn back from her neck, curled wildly. Marie pointed to the ring on Jane's finger.

"You wear it," she said to John and he nodded.

"It was her special ring. She gave it to me just before I left." How he misses her, Marie thought as she watched his face.

"What is that thing she is holding?" asked Samuel.

"Oh, that is Winston, her dog. Odd-looking, isn't he?"

"That cannot be a dog," scoffed Samuel. "This is a dog." Dog wagged his tail.

Marie passed the portrait back to John and he carefully rolled it and put it away. He picked up the charcoal and continued drawing. A long black braid hung over her shoulder, its end tied with beaded thongs. Shell earrings dangled from her earlobes. As he worked, John noticed for the first time the fine blue tattoos than ran around each of her wrists. Inside her left wrist, near the delicate blue tracings, was the image of some sort of insect.

He cleared his throat. "Those marks?" he asked. "What do they mean?"

How could she explain such a thing to him? She turned her wrists over and looked at her arms. There just below the base of her hand was the outline of a small blue dragonfly.

"The Miami wear the marks. My mother has far many more than I do, on her face and neck, but Père said this would do. It means that I am a woman amongst the People. Do girls in England not have this done?"

John sketched in the lines of the tattoos. Had he offended her? He realized that he knew little about girls or women, and he thought carefully as he spoke.

"No, they do different things," he answered slowly. What did they do? "A girl will wear different clothing or put up her hair. She goes to Court and is presented to the King and Queen. Then everyone knows that she is grown. My sister will do that some day." But is it really that simple? he asked himself. Jane has been to Court. Was she now a woman?

"We should have swum out to the ship," said Samuel. "We could have gone to the King." Marie did her best to ignore him, but Dog was listening closely.

"What is it like there in England?" asked Marie. John again paused in his drawing and looked into the fire. He had been gone for only a year, and yet that world seemed so very far away. He began to draw Marie's eyes. Their irises were a fine, deep green; the firelight brought out the small gold flecks in them.

"There are many more people. The villages and cities are crowded, and some towns like London are very large."

"Bigger than the fort?" asked Samuel in surprise.

"Oh, yes. Much bigger," laughed John.

"I do not believe this," snorted Samuel. "How can it be bigger than the fort?"

"London is an old place. People have been building on it for many years, hundreds of years. The buildings are stone and brick. The ladies are very grand. Some wear jewels in their hair, and their gowns have long skirts that trail on the ground behind them. They must have servants to carry the skirts. Some of the buildings, like the palace in which the King lives, have dozens of rooms."

"Does the King get lost in it?" asked Samuel seriously, and John laughed out loud to think of His Majesty King George wandering about in a castle calling for directions. Such a thing could never happen.

"No, he does not, but if he did, he has many servants to help him."

"Well, I would like to see it," said Marie. "I would like to walk in a house that has dozens of rooms, even if I did get lost." John tried to imagine Marie in London, her hair up, long satin skirts following her steps. He could not. She seemed too perfect here, he thought, and he felt his ears and neck grow warm.

"And Jane would like to come here. She wants to see the frontier."

"We will not do it, though," said Marie crossly. "She will stay there, and I will stay here. What sort of adventure is that?"

"I will go on a ship, then, and do it for both of you," Samuel declared, "and John will come with me. He can draw pictures of it all and send them. An eagle could carry them for us."

"First we must get back to the fort," said John. He carefully rolled up the unfinished drawing. "I need better light for this. Perhaps tomorrow."

"Tomorrow we will light fires on the beach," Marie said. "We will make them smoke with green branches. Someone will see and come for us." She did not seem worried, only sat poking at the fire now and again with a piece of wood. Samuel had found a small stick. He dangled his wig from it and held it close to the flames so it would dry more quickly.

"Do not drop it in," warned John. "If it burns, it will stink!"

"It stinks now," said Marie, wrinkling her nose, but Samuel ignored them both.

"That it does," said a voice from across the clearing, and all three young heads looked up. This island is becoming crowded, thought John.

# CHAPTER
# ELEVEN

A young man stood there. Straight, blond hair had escaped from a tie at the nape of his neck and hung in strings around his cheeks. He carried a musket. A carved powder horn and hunting pouch hung from his shoulder. A loose shirt was clinging damply to his frame, and his leggings and moccasins were stained and wet. There was a weathered handsomeness about him. He grinned broadly at the three young people. John recognized him as LaButte, the interpreter from the fort.

"Pierre!" shrieked Samuel, nearly dropping the wig into the flames. He ran to the man and caught him around the waist. Pierre hoisted the little boy up with one arm. Dog scrambled to his feet and barked happily. If Samuel was happy, Dog was happy.

"You grow heavy, Samuel. Soon you will pick me up. Marie Magdelaine Roy, you are well?" LaButte smiled when she looked him straight in the eyes as she always did when they spoke. He liked this girl who was so direct. She was not like other mademoiselles who could

barely get words out of their mouths and stared at the
ground in real or pretended shyness.

"I am well, monsieur," she said, and she smiled back.

LaButte turned his attention to John. "And you, young
MacNeil? The storm caught you here as well, I observe."

"We have not met, I think, sir," said John. "How do
you know who I am?"

"No, that is true, but I know of you," he answered.
"Everyone knows of you." This last was said by LaButte,
Marie, and Samuel all at once. Eyes widened and they all
laughed, even John. "The artist. You make the pictures."
LaButte held out his hand and John clasped it.

"He is drawing one of Marie," said Samuel in excitement. He slithered down out of LaButte's grasp. "Show
him, John."

"It is not finished yet," said John. "Tomorrow perhaps."
LaButte looked at him steadily, seriously for a moment,
and then broke into his quick smile.

"Yes. Perhaps tomorrow."

"There is food, Pierre, and a dry shirt," offered Marie
and she went quickly to the hanging basket. Pierre
followed Samuel to the wigwam for the clothing.

"How is it that you are on the island, Monsieur
LaButte? Is anyone else here?" asked John once the pair
emerged, and Pierre hung his damp shirt to dry. They all
sat down at the fire. Samuel tossed on more wood as
Pierre tore into the cold food Marie offered.

"No, I am alone. I had been out hunting and thought
to visit my orchard, you see. The day was fine, after all,

and then that storm. By the bells of Ste. Anne's, that was a blow!" He shook his head at the memory of the powerful wind.

"Ste. Anne's does not have bells," said Samuel. "But I will bring some back from England on my ship. Or the eagle might carry them."

Pierre looked confused for a moment. "Have I missed something?" he asked.

"No, it is just Samuel," said Marie, sighing. "Go on. Did you see the whirlwind?"

"Indeed, mademoiselle! I had to hold onto my canoe with my very teeth to keep her from sailing away into the air. I would wager those sailors on the *Swift* were doing the same thing."

"You saw the *Swift*! It was not damaged?" John asked hopefully.

"I would say no. She was flying down river with the current and the storm when I saw her pass. I was at the other end of Pêche, you see. How is it that you were not on her?"

Three pairs of eyes looked at John as he remembered his wild lunge for the escaping wig. How could he explain this without seeming like a fool? How could he say that he had fallen off the boat? He gave up.

"I fell off the boat." There was a stunned silence, then roars of laughter. John began laughing as well. What else could he do, after all?

"It can happen," said Pierre, nodding over his dinner. "The bateau goes one way and you go the other. It is worse with a canoe, *mon ami*."

"You will take us home?" asked Marie. She knew what his answer would be.

"It would be my honor, Mademoiselle Roy. And you, as well, John MacNeil. Samuel and his beast, though . . . they will have to swim alongside." Samuel pulled a face, but it was clear that he loved the teasing. Pierre finished his meal. He pulled the moccasins from his feet and set them near the fire to dry. Clad in the warm, dry shirt, he wiggled his bare toes in contentment.

They sat by the fire talking of all the things that had happened that afternoon. Marie wondered if the fort was safe and their parents unhurt. Pierre observed that a whirlwind could not knock down her father, the great Pierre Roy. The ship must be back there at the fort by now. Was a search party looking for them? They must go to the other side of the river soon and see the path that the storm had taken. John could draw the great trees that had been scattered like bits of straw. The fire popped a little; it was dying down. Then they became aware of a great silence in the night: Samuel's voice had stilled. His head had nodded down on his chest and he was asleep.

"This one is ready for his bed," said Pierre, and he moved to pick up the child in his arms to carry him into the wigwam.

"Leave him," said Marie softly. "I will cover him with a blanket. If he wakes in the night to find himself sleeping next to me in the wigwam he will be cross. He would want to sleep out here with the men." She slipped into the dark shelter and came back with three blankets. One she spread over Samuel, who had fallen over in a softly, snoring pile. Dog walked sleepily over, circled a few times, then curled into the crook of Samuel's bent legs. The other blankets she handed to John and Pierre.

"Sleep well," she said, and they wished her the same. Then she disappeared into the wigwam. Its flaps slipped down, and for a moment there was only the soft rustling of the wind in the trees.

"Good night, Monsieur LaButte," said John.

"*Bonne nuit*," said Pierre quietly. "And it is Pierre. To sleep then, John MacNeil. The sunrise comes early tomorrow." They settled themselves near the fire.

John thought about Marie. Samuel had been left to sleep out here with the men, she had said. No one had ever spoken of him this way — perhaps those green eyes saw him differently. Could she be the person with whom he might some day share his life? Marie had been friendly and warm. For now the friendship was enough. John lay there thinking about Marie and her long, dark braid. He thought he would never fall asleep, but before he knew it, worn out by the storm, he was sleeping soundly.

Loud bird song broke into his dreams and John slowly woke, not exactly certain where he was. Although his eyes were still shut, John had a strange feeling that someone was looking at him. Jane, of course. Was she in his room again?

"Did you hear the bears last night?" whispered Samuel, and John's eyes snapped open. The boy's face was inches from his own.

"There are no bears on this island," said John as he stretched.

"So you say," argued Samuel. John sat up. Warm shafts of sunlight shone through the trees, and the wind was still blowing hard.

"If bears had come, Samuel, and seen you, they would have run off in deadly fear of their lives," said Pierre. He was pulling on his moccasins. "*Bon matin*, John MacNeil." Marie had just come out of the wigwam, braiding her hair as she walked. Dog rolled on his back in the sandy soil, grunting contentedly.

"Good morning," she said. John watched her step across the pools of sunshine that dappled the camp. Her slim fingers worked quickly and her hair soon draped down her back in a smooth, shining braid. She tied its end with the leather thong. Her tanned cheeks were flushed and her green eyes smiled. John thought of the drawing in his case. When would he have the time to finish it? Perhaps he could ask her to pose when they were back at the fort.

"I'm hungry," called Samuel. He was examining the wig. It was dry now, but it had taken on a very strange shape. He seemed pleased with it just the same.

"There is not much for breakfast. Do you wish to hunt or fish, or do you wish to eat what we have and start for home?"

"Let's eat what we have, Marie." Samuel was trying on the wig. First backwards with the tail hanging in his face, then correctly, which looked not much better.

"Well then, there is the gallette and apples. I confess

we borrowed a few, Pierre." She went back to the hanging basket where the food had been safely stored for the night. She reached inside and took out the bread and the small apples.

"As long as it is only a few," he scolded with mock fierceness, shaking his finger at her.

Marie smiled at his teasing. "Will you have one, Pierre?" she asked, holding out an apple. He inclined his head a bit, then took it from her.

"*Merci*," he said, and he slowly bit into the fruit.

"And you, John." He took his breakfast from her and watched as she gave the dog some gallette.

"This makes me think of a story," said Samuel, helping himself to an apple and gallette.

"Naturally," said John, nodding his thanks to Marie, who was eating a piece of the flat bread. They all sat on the stones around the firepit. A little of last night's warmth still rose from the ashes.

"It is the one about the woman who gave the apple to the man. There is an evil lizard in it. No, a snake, and the snake guards the apples." Marie felt the urge to gag her brother.

"Ho! Adam and Eve," said Pierre. "Very amusing, my young scamp. You need someone to guard you." Pierre finished his breakfast and kicked sand over the ashes of the fire.

"Get what you want to take home, Samuel. No stories now — put on your moccasins. The wind still blows very hard, and it will not make the river crossing any easier," said Marie. She put away the empty basket, and took the folded blankets inside the wigwam. She bundled their dry clothing from yesterday and stuffed it into a leather bag, which she flung across her back. Bringing two wooden canteens from the wigwam, she filled them with water from the canal. Pierre had his musket and gear, John hung his document case from his shoulder, and Samuel was wearing his precious wig. They were ready.

Pierre led the way out of the camp. For a while they followed the canal. It widened and narrowed and twisted through the island. Red-winged blackbirds scolded from the other side where they nested in the reeds that grew in the shallows. Cicadas sang in the growing warmth, and great rushes of wind hissed through the huge, old trees. Their branches hung low over the water. Once or twice they heard the plop of a muskrat diving for shelter.

Samuel ran ahead of his sister, and slipped his small hand into Pierre's. That left Marie picking her way through the grass just ahead of John. Now and again she flipped back her heavy braid. The black hair gleamed in the sunlight. John could see a small mole just at the side of the base of her neck above the edge of her shirt.

Marie turned suddenly and John hoped she had not caught him staring. She dropped back until they were walking side by side. John felt a strange confusion. He liked the fact that she was walking next to him and yet he suddenly felt awkward. He hoped she would not ask him anything.

"When we are home you must come to my father's house," she said. "It would be a good place to finish the picture. Do you not think so?"

Say something clever, he told himself. Do not sound like an idiot. "Yes," he answered, and the word caught in his throat.

"Have you swallowed an insect?" asked Marie. "Well, it will not hurt you." And she smiled to herself.

"Yes. That is to say, no, I have not swallowed an insect and yes, I will come to your father's home to finish the picture. Or you might come to the fort."

"If you go to the fort, then I come as well!" shrieked Samuel. "You may be able to escape Mère and Père, but you will never escape me."

"I suppose I will not," Marie said under her breath, and John laughed.

"Now, Samuel, do not eavesdrop on two friends when they talk. It is most rude. Do you not agree, John MacNeil?" And Pierre glanced back at John and Marie.

"Oh, yes. Most rude," agreed John. "But if you do come to the fort, Samuel, and I say *if*, for I could not welcome you if you were rude, then I will show you the *Swift*." Samuel released Pierre's hand and ran back to John.

"I will have manners. I will be good. I want to see it. Can we sail on the bateau?"

"*Touché*, John MacNeil. You have made a friend for life," said Pierre without looking back. His spine was straight and the set of his shoulders suddenly seemed slightly stiff. Marie watched him. What was this, now? She quickened her pace until she walked next to Pierre.

"We are all friends, I would hope," she said to him.

"Is that what you hope, mademoiselle?" he asked,

looking at her steadily. "Friends?" Marie did not know how to answer.

"She has swallowed an insect," whispered Samuel in a very loud whisper. "A large one." But they had come clear of the woods and Pierre seemed to forget his question. Samuel raced out onto the beach. A northerly wind was blowing briskly and large whitecaps rose and fell all over the lake and river. John could see that they were only halfway down the island. They would walk along the shore until they reached the spot where Pierre had hidden his canoe.

"He is so much like my sister when she was that age," John said.

"In what way?" asked Marie. She stopped for a moment and took off her moccasins so that she could walk in the water. John and Pierre waited for her.

"Well," said John as they started again. "Like him she never stops talking. She is interested in everything and she is full of odd plans."

"Yes, that is Samuel," agreed Marie. She held up her skirt just a little so its hem would stay dry.

"But she is like you as well," continued John. "It is the strangest thing. Perhaps it is only that you are both girls. Women, I should say. You talk about the same things."

"What are those things?" asked Pierre, who felt a little left out. "Marriage and babies and the home?" He was on safe ground now. All women loved those topics.

"Adventure," said John. He stooped to pick up a small crab claw. It was pink and delicately edged with salmon.

He uncapped the case and dropped it in. It would have been more satisfying to sink down onto the sand and draw it now, but they must go on.

"Adventure?" wondered Pierre aloud, but he dared not tease Marie too thoroughly. She had a temper, that one.

"Yes," said John, conscious of Pierre's eyes on him as he spoke to Marie. "Neither one of you think that you know any excitement. You think your lives are ordinary."

"My life is ordinary," said Marie as she kicked through the waves that washed up on the beach. "Nothing happens here, you see." She had John's attention now.

"Jane says the same thing," he laughed. "She goes to Court and speaks with the King but she wants to come here. You have more freedom than any young woman in England would ever have. You do as you please, but you wish to see England. You must trade places. I would like to see that!"

"And I would like to see Fort Detroit, so we must step a little more quickly," Pierre said a bit shortly. "My canoe is just ahead. Samuel with his eagle eyes has spotted it." The boy and Dog were far down the beach. Samuel waved his arms over his head and gestured in some bizarre code he seemed to be making up.

They drew closer and John could see the canoe. Pierre had wedged it between some small trees. No wind could have moved the thing. He helped Pierre ease it out from its resting place and together they carried it to the water's edge. A few steps farther and it was floating, an end pointing at the river.

"You first, John MacNeil, at the bow." John carefully

climbed in. "And you, Samuel, just behind him." Samuel did as Pierre told him as Dog leaped in as well. "And now you, Marie. Careful now, we will hold it steady. You do not wish to fall in."

"I have climbed into a canoe before, Monsieur LaButte. I have, well, *had* one of my own."

"Ah, yes, Mademoiselle Roy, a lapse of my memory. You shall have another soon. I am certain of it."

John turned and watched Pierre's face. He had spent the summer studying faces, for he did not only draw a mouth and a nose and a pair of eyes. There was more to a portrait than the shape of the chin or the color of the hair. John had learned to watch for feelings. He had drawn officers with their haughty expressions and volunteers from the militia, bristling under unwelcome orders. His sketches showed the eyes of men filled with greed and the shoulders of women slumped with discouragement at the never-ending work and worry that faced them in this dangerous place. What he saw in Pierre's eyes surprised him, and yet perhaps it should not have. He is in love with her, John thought. And she does not know it.

With them all settled in the canoe, Pierre said, "There's a paddle next to you, Marie, and one near you, monsieur." Pierre quickly gave the canoe a shove and hopped in as well. All three began to paddle hard. The canoe drew away from Pêche Island. The sound of their paddle strokes faded from the beach, and in moments even Samuel's complaint that he was the only one without a paddle drifted into the wind and disappeared.

# CHAPTER
# TWELVE

They paddled hard and soon fell into a steady rhythm.
John thought that Samuel would be wriggling around,
leaning over and trailing his hands in the water. But
Samuel sat straight and still. From the time he was a tiny
baby he had ridden in canoes with his father and mother.
Here he behaved. Dog sat close to him, shifting his
weight as the canoe rose and fell on the choppy waves,
sniffing endlessly at the enticing odors that only he could
smell. Spray sparkled in the sun and flecked John's arms
as he paddled. His shirt was soon damp, but he was
hot and sweaty with the paddling and it felt wonderful
to him.

The current was strong, as much as three knots here,
John's father had told him. The *Swift*, or even a sailing
canoe, had to have a strong breeze blowing from across
or behind to make way upstream. To sail or paddle
upwind was slow going and sometimes impossible. But
today they were fortunate and a steady wind would help
them on their way home. Pierre steered the canoe,
changing their course now so that they moved directly

downstream. Land and trees flew by on either side. Still, they were at least three leagues from the fort. It would be some time until they were there.

"We have visitors," shouted Pierre above the wind, but under his breathe he cursed. "I knew this was too easy." John looked over his shoulder. Behind them in the distance were three canoes. He faced the bow again and continued paddling, struggling to fall back into a rhythm with the others.

"Who are they?" asked Marie, glancing back uneasily with wide green eyes.

"I am not certain," called Pierre. "We will know when they catch us."

That sent a thrill of discomfort through John. He had heard many stories of what happened when you were caught and taken in this country. You might be sold as a slave and end your days deep in an uncharted part of the wilderness — that or worse. He turned his head around again. The canoes were already closer. All three were much bigger than Pierre's. Many men rode in each of them as their paddle strokes rose and fell relentlessly.

"I think they are war canoes, Pierre!" cried Samuel, forgetting the strict rules of behavior. "Yes! They are war canoes!"

Pierre looked back quickly. The boy, unfortunately, was correct; now he could see the painted hulls. By the pews of Ste. Anne's, they were quick! He made his decision.

"We will head for the shore. Paddle hard now, all of you!"

"But Pierre, they will catch us on the land," cried Marie. As Pierre turned the canoe back into the chop, the war canoes turned as well, angling toward them. John could clearly see the designs on the hulls. The warriors' muscles flexed as they paddled. Sweat dripped from their painted faces.

"They will catch us anyway, Marie. Better on land than out here on the water."

"Can you tell who they are?" shouted John. The canoes drew about ten lengths away then stayed in line with them, coming no closer.

"They are Odawas." But Pierre could not understand this. What were these men doing here in war canoes? The Odawas lived in a village that was across the river from the fort. They came there to trade as other tribes did, but this was no group of traders. Pierre kept his fears to himself.

All four of them now faced straight ahead as though some voice had commanded it. Marie lifted her chin slightly as she dipped her paddle into the water. John and Pierre paddled with hard strokes. Samuel was motionless and silent. Even Dog turned his muzzle into the wind and lifted his pointed, gray ears as though they were the only vessel on the river. The Odawas did not once glance over as their canoes surged through the water.

Then they were at the north shore of the mainland. Pierre and Marie back-paddled to slow the canoe. John vaulted out and grasping the prow, eased the vessel to the shore. Pierre climbed out. The three war canoes landed alongside them with a hiss, and the Odawas began to spill from them.

"Stay where you are," said Pierre quietly to Marie and Samuel in French. Then to the Odawas in their own tongue, "Greetings. Have you come far?"

"Far enough. We will go farther before we lay down our paddles." John watched the man who had spoken. He had cool, black eyes set deeply in his face. Like all the others in his party, his hair had been shaved from his ears forward. His long topknot was pulled back and held with thongs and feathers. He wore only a breech cloth and low, beaded moccasins. His head and body were painted red and black. A carved wooden tomahawk and a knife hung from a belt that circled his waist. John could see trade muskets in the canoes, but each man had a bow and a quiver of arrows slung across his shoulders as well. They have left nothing to chance, he thought.

"I am LaButte, translator for Pontiac with the British. We are on our way back to Fort Detroit," said Pierre. "And you? Where is your chief?"

The Odawa only smiled at this. "I am Oyan. My chief? You will see soon enough," he answered. Then without taking his eyes off Pierre, he called something to his men. Six warriors seized the canoe's sides, motioning that they would pull it up the beach. John staggered back out of their way. One of the Odawas reached for Samuel, but Marie grabbed Samuel's hand and pulled him from the canoe. Dog was beside them in a moment.

"Do not touch him," she hissed in Miami. They will understand, she knew. The two tongues were close enough. Her heart was pounding and she felt a weakness in her knees. Dog, who had followed Samuel, stood by

Marie's legs growling softly. The men grinned and some laughed a little at this bristling young woman. This one had no fear.

"You have no reason to stop us," said Pierre. "We have business at the fort, I tell you." Men were moving past him, already heading away from the river.

"That is of no matter," answered Oyan. "Now you will come with us." The warriors were dragging Pierre's canoe up onto the beach and into the bushes. He snatched up his musket as it passed by and Marie grabbed up the canteens. The Odawas made no move to prevent them, which made it all stranger than ever.

"Does Pontiac tell his warriors to stop peaceful travelers?" challenged Pierre.

"Ask him yourself when we get to his camp," answered Oyan, enjoying the expression on the Frenchman's face.

Pierre paused in surprise. "He is here, you say?" And he felt the cold stone of fear that had rested in his belly ease a little. "Come," he said to Marie, Samuel, and John in French. "We must go with them."

They fell in with the warriors. All the canoes were now beached and hidden. A few men stayed behind to watch them and the river. Into the bushes and the forest they went in single file. Marie did not hold Samuel's hand. He must walk on his own; he was not a little child at this moment. Dog, however, did not seem to think the same way. He padded along close to Samuel, now and again leaning his gray body against the boy.

"Is it far?" asked Samuel suddenly, and John groaned to himself. Jane might as well have come along. Oyan's eyes flicked over the boy. If it had been a man who had asked, if it had been someone who quaked in fear, he would not have answered. But Samuel just looked back steadily, waiting for his answer.

"Not so far. You are young and your legs look strong. Two days' walking will be nothing to you." Samuel could understand most of what Oyan said, and he repeated it to John. Where are we going? John wondered. What could they want with us? But Oyan did not say more.

Pierre chuckled as he settled his musket across his arms more comfortably. "You all wanted excitement?" he said. "Well, you shall have it!"

And he laughed to himself as they disappeared in the deep, cool forest.

# CHAPTER
# THIRTEEN

From the direction of the sun, John could tell that they were taking a path roughly parallel to the river and away from Detroit. Once in the forest beyond the water, it felt much warmer. Huge maple and beech trees blocked out the stiff north wind. In the deep woods, there was little underbrush and the walking was fairly easy. Now and then they broke from the trees into a clearing. Goldenrod, cornflowers, and wild carrot waved in the wind. Clouds of butterflies — yellow, orange, white, and purple — fluttered from blossom to blossom. The air was thick with the buzzing of bees and the sleepy drone of cicadas.

John did not have a sense of danger, but he felt he must ask. "Are we prisoners, do you think, Pierre?"

"Not exactly. The word *guests* comes to my mind. A bit reluctant, perhaps, but still guests." They walked until the sun was high in the sky. Then Oyan called something to the warriors and the line of men disbanded. A small stream flowed nearby, and groves of ash trees cast cool shade on its mossy banks.

"We will stop here, but not for long," said Oyan. "And only because of the child." He liked the boy's brave way, but he could not say as much. He had a small son of his own, although his wife had died last winter. He hoped his son would be as strong if taken by others.

Everyone unshouldered their packs and dropped to the ground. Oyan was true to his word. No sooner had they sat in the shade and sipped from the canteens or the stream, than they were up and walking once more. This time it was not until the sun dappled the forest floor with pink light and sunset approached that Oyan called a halt. The Odawas exchanged words and some men disappeared into the forest.

"They will hunt for our meal," he said. Then he turned to look steadily at Marie. "Make a fire." She did not move, but only stared back, her arms folded across her chest.

"I think he is talking to you, Marie," said Samuel cheerfully. He did like to be helpful. Perhaps Marie had not heard the Odawa correctly.

"I know he is talking to me," answered Marie stiffly. "But I am not a servant."

"We are not in a position to argue here, Marie," said John. He did not understand Oyan's words, but the message was clear. "Come, Samuel, let us gather sticks. I for one do not wish to eat raw meat." Samuel trotted along next to him, and Dog, who would not be left behind, followed the boy. When they came back, they carried tinder, sticks, and a few branches. Moments later, her face set, Marie struck flint against steel to start a fire.

It was not long before the men returned with game. There were rabbits and a fat young doe. They quickly skinned the animals and cut branches for stakes upon which to grill the meat. The smells of wood smoke and cooking food soon rose in the warm, late afternoon air.

The camp was not silent. The Odawas talked and joked amongst themselves; they seemed to think that Samuel with his wig was very amusing. John could only guess at what they said. When the meat was blackened and juices dripped into the fire, the stakes were pulled off one by one. It might not have been the most finely seasoned dinner in the world — it was a bit tough and a few hairs stuck to it here and there — but to John's empty stomach after the long day's march, it was a banquet. Even Dog gnawed contentedly on scraps and one of the bones.

After they finished eating, the Odawas set aside some food for the morning. John washed his greasy hands and face in the stream that ran beyond the camp, wiped his palms on his shirttails, and returned to where the others sat at the small fire across from Oyan and his men.

"What will happen?" he quietly asked Pierre. "If we are not prisoners, why have we been taken in this way?" Pierre lay on the grass, propped up on an elbow. His musket was close by. Marie and Samuel watched him silently and waited for his answer. Dog delicately licked at the thigh bone of the doe; he cared nothing for all of this.

"What do you know of Pontiac?" asked Pierre.

John shook his head and shrugged his shoulders. "I know only a little, what they talk of at the fort. Pontiac

is the chief of the Odawas." John pulled a stalk of timo-
thy grass and nibbled at its tender green tip. "They say
little of the Odawas, though, no more than what they
say of other tribes. They come to trade and then
they leave again. I do not believe that Captain Campbell
thinks too much of it all. Why would he worry? There
are soldiers and cannons defending the place."

"And why would that be, that he does not worry?"
asked Pierre, although he knew differently. "Does he
think that Pontiac and his influence are not a force
here? Does he think the tribes would not ever threaten
Detroit? No, *mon ami*, you are wrong. Campbell knows
how restless these people are."

John said nothing for the moment. LaButte was an
interpreter there. He had Campbell's ear and was friendly
with the chiefs to whom he spoke. But Pierre did not
spend his life in the company of the British officers. He
did not sit down to dinner with them now and again
and listen to what they said over Madeira and their pipes.
But then John remembered how some conversations had
ended rather suddenly when he entered a room. Could
they have been keeping their suspicions from him? John
reluctantly acknowledged that Pierre must be right.
Perhaps he had not always been meant to hear what was
being spoken. If only Jane had been here. No secret would
have escaped her.

"Père says that there is word that orders have been
given to refuse powder to the tribes who trade at the
fort," said Marie very quietly. She glanced at Samuel who
had stood and wandered over to the other side of the

fire. Dog dropped his bone. His slanting, yellow eyes were fastened on the child and his body was tense. Now Samuel was letting one of the Odawas examine his wig. She did not wish to frighten her little brother with all of this talk; perhaps it was well that he had moved away from what they were saying.

"Captain Campbell makes gifts to them now and again," said John. He saw Samuel talking to Oyan. What could they be saying, with only so much language between them?

"Campbell means well with his gifts, but it will not be enough, I think. Not many use just the bow and spear to get food and furs. The old ways are gone forever," said Pierre. "We all must have muskets and ammunition to survive. There are those who look back to how things were when the French had the fort." Now he watched Samuel as well.

Marie stood suddenly and walked to her brother. The warriors all looked up as she crossed to the other side of the fire where they lay, smoking and relaxing. John wondered at how calm and steady she was.

"Come, Samuel," she said in French. She took his hand. "It has been a long day and you must sleep soon."

"Leave the boy," Oyan replied with a ghost of a smile. John stiffened in surprise as Pierre grinned at the Odawa's words. The man had answered her in French, the strange, accentless French that many Natives spoke, but it was French nonetheless. "He only wishes to spend time with warriors." How many languages did the man know? John asked himself. It was a strange place, Canada. As soon as you thought you understood something or someone, you were proven wrong. Oyan was watching Marie. She met his eyes, though not in defiance.

"He must sleep. We have walked all day and you set a quick pace. Or will we go more slowly tomorrow?" Oyan drew on his pipe and then blew the smoke out into the night. He ran a hand over his smoothly shaved head and looked up at the sky as though he was considering her question.

"It is a wise choice — a young boy needs to sleep. Rest then. We do have far to walk tomorrow." He turned away from her and fell into low conversation with his men.

Samuel went docilely back with Marie. She lay down and pulled him close to her. He did not protest; it had indeed been a long, tense day. Dog padded over and curled up against them both. John and Pierre settled themselves as best they could. John lay his head on his document case. He had never thought months ago in England that he would ever be using it for a pillow.

The fire snapped and quiet settled over the camp. Then John heard Marie speak to her brother in a voice that was less than a whisper.

"Whatever did you talk of with him, Samuel?" The little boy snuggled down into his sister's arms. When he answered, his voice was sleepy and slow.

"We talked about you, Marie." Then he fell asleep.

# CHAPTER
# FOURTEEN

They rose with the sun and ate a cold meal of leftover game as they sat around the dead fire. John wondered whether he had dreamed what Samuel had said. He couldn't ask him, however. There was no time. Almost before they had begun to arrange their sleep-rumpled clothing and pick up their belongings, they were again on the march through the forest.

In the night the wind had died. The clear, dry air was gone and the usual humid heat of summer had returned. It was windless and close and as the morning turned into midday, John's clothing began to stick to him. He ignored this. His wanderings with Wallace and Natka had usually left little time for preening. Still, a swim would be grand at the moment. He thought of the two men with whom he had spent so much time. Were they looking for him? Did his father believe him dead from the storm and the river?

Today they did not stop but kept a steady pace. Pierre and then John picked up Samuel and carried him for a while. Marie did the same, but the boy was too heavy for her. They passed their canteens around. Water would have to do, since the Odawas did not offer more food. Then, several of the warriors broke from the line and ran on ahead, whooping and calling in their own language. The others laughed and talked loudly. There were answering cries from ahead.

"We must be close to their camp," said John. He peered through the trees and bushes, pushing aside branches as he walked. They entered a clearing. Smoke from fires scented the air. Many warriors stood or sat in groups. John was conscious of dozens of eyes set in painted, expressionless faces watching him. There were some curious mutters, but no one made a move against them.

"Steady," Pierre said quietly. They crossed the clearing with Oyan leading them. He held his head high, walking in proud silence through the camp. Oyan stopped before a man who was seated on a blanket near one of the fires. It was Pontiac.

John would always remember his first sight of the chief. He would see him once again. He would hear terrible tales of what eventually came to happen at Detroit and all up and down the lakes, but this first image would stay lodged in his memory forever.

Pontiac was not a big man and he did not look that much different from the other Odawas who filled the clearing. His head was shaved and tattoos covered his skin. His face was painted in red and black designs. Heavy earrings of copper and bone dangled from his lobes; a medicine bag and a knife in a quilled sheath hung around his neck. He wore a simple breech cloth and low, beaded moccasins. He might have been one of a thousand Natives — Odawa, Potawatomi, Huron, or Delaware — who passed through Fort Detroit's gates or slid past the fort going up or down the river in canoes. It was his eyes that made him seem different. Deep and black, they watched the proceedings with a silky disdain that even Lieutenant Jeffrey Lindsay could never have matched. For a moment John thought he saw something shine in their depths. A gleam of the most pure, clear hatred flickered there. Then it was gone.

John stood with the others. The Odawas stepped back, waiting to see what would happen. Oyan said something to Pontiac in their own tongue. As he talked and Pontiac answered, Pierre began to translate into French for them, whispering each phrase softly just a moment after it was spoken.

"Greetings, Pontiac," said Oyan in a clear voice.

"Greetings to you, Oyan," answered Pontiac, and he gestured for the other man to sit. "I see you have brought some new guests to our fires."

"I have, Pontiac," said Oyan as he settled in the grass next to his chief. "You know at least one of them, but they all call the fort their home."

"This is good. I thank you, Oyan. I have not spoken for some time with LaButte. Yet another council, is it? How simple things were before the English came." Then he turned his eyes upon Pierre and smiled the slightest bit.

"Welcome, LaButte! I did not think to see you here so far from the fort and your apple trees."

"I did not think to be here, Pontiac. It is your warrior Oyan who was so thoughtful. You must reward him for his hospitality." Now they were both speaking Odawa. Marie took up translating where Pierre had stopped, but she could only repeat a rough idea of what they said.

"I will do this," answered Pontiac with casual grace, and he turned to Oyan. "Think on it, my friend, then ask for what you will." Oyan glared at Pierre, but nodded thanks to the chief from where he sat across from him at the fire. Pontiac seemed to relax even more. His lids drooped and he slumped a little.

"Come and sit, LaButte. Tell me, who are these young ones?" Pierre gestured for them to move forward, then he lowered himself, cross-legged, to the ground. John, Marie, and Samuel came forward and did the same. Dog lay down close to Samuel. Marie fell silent and for a while, John could only guess at what was spoken.

"The boy is Samuel, son of Pierre Roy. The girl is his sister Marie, daughter of Margeurite Ouabankikove, of the Miami." Pontiac nodded slowly. John looked sideways at Marie. She sat there, as still as though she had been carved from wood, her eyes lowered. This was not the Marie he had come to know.

"I knew her grandfather, Many Birds. He could snare more geese than anyone else in less time. What a hunter he was!" remembered Pontiac. "Who is the other?"

"He is John MacNeil, son of Captain James MacNeil at Fort Detroit. He fell from the bateau of the Scotsman Doig, and we found him on Pêche Island." Pontiac said nothing for a moment, then he slapped his thighs and burst into loud laughter. John could not be quiet any longer.

"What did you say? Why is he laughing?" he asked Pierre, looking from one man to the other.

"I told him you fell off of Doig's bateau."

John rolled his eyes hopelessly. "Thank you, Pierre. I am so pleased that everyone on the frontier now knows of this."

Pontiac continued to laugh softly and he shook his head. The English. What could he say?

"Bring food," he called, chuckling. "We will have a feast, I think, in honor of these guests!"

John saw that a meal was already underway on fires throughout the camp. Meat broiled and steam rose from pots. There were some women here, but not as many as would have been in a village. There were no children and not even a single dog wandered through the encampment. Samuel's Dog was the only animal to be seen. This was a temporary camp, then, John realized. He knew that the Odawa village lay across the river from Detroit, a little downstream. Why were they here? he wondered.

◇ ◇

Some warriors were eating from communal pots as they sat around the fires. Pigeons were grilling on stakes over the coals. The woods were filled with these birds; John had seen endless flocks of them darkening the skies. People did not bother to shoot them — they just knocked them out of their roosts in trees with a long stick. Kettles of meat and corn or onions and fish were served around. Everybody ate from these with their hands. John's fingers and palms were soon greasy and he wiped his hands on the grass near him. Most of the Odawas wiped their fingers in their hair. John wondered what Jane would think of this. It surpassed even Lord Elgie's habits at table.

The meal did not really end. Pots of food were left out to be picked over by anyone who felt like nibbling a little more. The fires began to die down to beds of coals that glowed with each breath of wind. Pipes were lit and conversations rumbled in the evening air.

"You were on the small island then, LaButte," said Pontiac suddenly. He lit a pipe and solemnly passed it to Pierre. Pierre drew on the pipe once and then passed it back to the chief, who offered it to Oyan. The smell of burning tobacco drifted to John's nostrils. He could not understand what they were saying, and Marie did not translate. She sat quietly, her hands in her lap, the blue dragonfly bright on her wrist, and watched Samuel feed Dog bites of pigeon.

"Yes, I have apple trees there. Someday I may build a house on that island. It would be a fine place to live, I think."

Pontiac nodded his agreement as he blew a fragrant puff of smoke into the night. "Yes, it is a good place. I go there sometimes to pray when I must make a hard decision. I was there not long ago." Pontiac stared into the fire.

"But you are here now, my friend," said Pierre quietly. "Have you made your decision?" Marie looked up at the men. John watched her set face closely.

"What are they saying?" he asked Marie softly. Pontiac drew on his pipe. He looked up at the stars that were just beginning to twinkle. As he spoke, Marie whispered his words as well as she could understand them.

"I think that someday there will be as many English in this land as there are stars in the sky," he said, ignoring Pierre's question. "You French were one thing. You traded fairly. You made the correct gifts to show your respect as one must. But these English have no respect. They will not even trade the guns and powder and balls that we need. I have made my decision."

John felt a great discomfort at what Marie whispered.

"They are a hard people, the English, it is true," mused Pierre. "What will you do, Pontiac?"

"Do you think that I do not have eyes on every tree and stream in this land? Word comes to me from everywhere, LaButte. There will be another council. I will wait here to speak with other chiefs before we listen to the English. Even now, the new English Major is at the fort. Oh, I know how it will go. The English will make more promises. If they are not kept . . ." His words trailed off.

John listened to Marie's whispers. He had heard rumors of a harder, more strict rule coming to Detroit, but nothing that Campbell or his father would share with him, or even discuss in his hearing. Until yesterday he had not thought that the trading policies at the fort had been so unfair. How could he have missed the sense of contempt with which the Odawa and others were being treated? He thought of Natka, his close friend. There was a respect between them that did not need words. It could have been no other way.

"Tell him something for me, Pierre," said John suddenly. Pontiac looked over at John, a hint of a smile playing around his straight, hard mouth.

"You must take care what you say, John. He is a great chief," warned Pierre.

"Tell him I know he is a great chief. Tell him not all English are the same. He has welcomed me to his fire and given me good food, even though he does not feel any love for my people. Tell him I wish to give him a gift."

Pierre studied John, his eyes narrowing. The boy had nerve. Then he turned to Pontiac and spoke. The chief drew on his pipe once more. Many of the warriors were listening, and the camp had grown quiet. Flames popped and snapped; sparks lifted into the air. Pontiac watched John for a moment, then he nodded.

"Let the boy make his gift." Pierre spoke for them both, first French for John and then Odawa for Pontiac.

"I would like to draw you, if you will let me." John looked at Pontiac as he spoke to Pierre. "That is my gift to you. I can make a picture of a great chief and send it to King George in England. I am his artist here in Canada. Surely if he sees you, he will know that you and your people deserve the respect you have not been given up to now." Pierre sighed at John's simple view of things. Only one so young could think to change the world of war and trade.

"Perhaps," said Pontiac. "Perhaps not. But I will let you make a picture."

"Excellent," said John with excitement, after Pierre translated. "I will need good light, Samuel. Bring more wood and build up the fire." The little boy set off with Dog at his heels. He had barely said a word or moved a muscle, so struck was he by the camp and Pontiac's men. It was good to get up and stretch. Soon the fire's flames were giving off a bright golden light as the snap and pop of sparks rose up into the darkness above them.

John uncapped his case and pulled out his paper, charcoals, and terra cotta chalk. He smoothed the rolled paper and began to draw. A few warriors crept up behind him and stood watching over his shoulders as Pontiac's image began to appear. John was barely conscious of their murmurs. He sketched the face and the shape of the shoulders, then glanced up at his model.

Pontiac had drawn a striped blanket around himself against the evening air. John created the ripples and folds in which it fell. He added each detail, sketching in the jewelry, the ornamented hair, the proud expression. The eyes he left for last. They had to be exactly right. He stopped drawing for a moment and looked at Pontiac, who met his gaze. They stared at each other across a distance greater than any John might have imagined. How could one person be so different from another? He bent back over his work; for a long while he drew. Then he straightened and smiled. Behind him the warriors nodded and rumbled approval. The image of Pontiac was there on the paper, as true as a reflection in a still pond.

John stood and walked to Pontiac. He crouched next to the chief and showed him the picture. Pontiac looked down at it. He saw himself, proud and unsmiling. In the eyes was understanding, a look of defiance. They were the eyes of a man who could see the future and knew what he believed that he must do.

"You will leave tomorrow morning," he said to John as he passed back the drawing. "When you send this to your king, he will see that I mean the words I will say to his soldiers at the fort."

Oyan had watched all of this with no comment. He had remained seated when many others had stood behind the boy to watch him draw. His thoughts were on other matters. Now he spoke.

"You offered me a gift for bringing these guests to your fire, Pontiac. I have thought on it," he said as all eyes turned to him.

"You are an able warrior, Oyan. You have always been loyal, standing by my side in all things. What would you have, my friend? A musket? A fine tomahawk?" Pierre quietly translated.

"None of those things. I would take a wife again. You know it has been my plan for a time. When the Frenchman and the others leave here tomorrow, I wish the woman Marie to stay. She is strong and brave and would do well with us." Pierre stiffened in surprise. He dared say nothing to Pontiac at this moment.

"Tell me he did not say what I believe he said," whispered Marie hotly. "I will not do it!"

"Calm, Marie. We must play this thing out," Pierre

urged softly. John watched her angry face, the flushed cheeks, and blazing eyes. How could this be happening? Pontiac regarded Marie for a moment, then he nodded.

"It will be so, then," said Pontiac in agreement, and in helpless confusion, Pierre repeated his words to them all. "She has no man, after all. She will be yours and it will be a good match, I think."

"But she does have a man, Pontiac, so she cannot be given to another," said John suddenly. Pierre repeated his words. What did the boy have planned?

"Is she yours then?" asked Oyan in surprise. He had not considered this. "Is she promised to you?"

John hesitated before he spoke. For a moment his parents and their sometimes reserved marriage came into his mind. They might not see eye to eye on all things; they had disagreed on his fate here, but at least they had chosen each other as marriage partners. Jane and Henry had done the same thing. In time he as well would find someone to share his life.

Marie's head snapped around and she stared at John. He saw something new in her eyes. All along, the slightest idea that perhaps Marie could have been the one for him had played in his mind. If he spoke now and claimed her as his betrothed before all these people, she might come to see herself in that way. But then he remembered the expression on Pierre's face as he had helped Marie into the canoe that morning. We are all friends, she had said.

"No, she is not promised to me. She is with Pierre." Pierre was so shocked that for a second he could barely translate.

"This is so?" Oyan said to Marie. She looked across at Pierre. She had always thought of him only as her father's friend. He had often been around at the house or in the fields, and he almost seemed like one of their family, an older brother perhaps. When she was little he had treated her like a child, swinging her in the air when she ran to meet him, as he did with Samuel now. He had not done that for quite a while. He spoke to her with a quiet warmth that she should have noticed before this night. How hard it would be not to see him again if she were married to another. In a rush, Marie knew that she did not ever want that to happen.

"It is so," she said to Oyan, and she knew she was speaking the truth. "I am with Pierre." The Odawa nodded his understanding. That was it, then. He wanted a wife, a partner in his life, not a prisoner.

"Perhaps a fine tomahawk will be better after all," he said to Pontiac with amusement, knowing that Marie understood his words. A little put out to hear herself compared to a weapon, Marie still kept her mouth closed.

Samuel could not bear it a moment more. He had been good. He had not wandered through the camp chatting with the warriors. He had not asked to handle their war clubs. He had not even told one single story! He had behaved himself, but this endless talk about kings and Marie and Pierre had stretched his control to its limits.

"What is going on?" he asked. "Is somebody getting married? Is that what I heard you say?" Pierre laughed, John sighed with relief, and Marie, amazingly enough, blushed to the roots of her thick, black hair.

"Time will tell, *mon petit*," said Pierre to the little boy. "Time will tell."

# CHAPTER
# FIFTEEN

The next morning they left. Warriors and chiefs from other tribes had arrived during the night. More were drifting into the clearing now. A few questioning, hot glances came their way, but no one challenged them.

"Do not forget, young Englishman," Pontiac said to John as Pierre translated. "Tell your king that my patience with the ways of his officers and traders is at an end."

"I will remember," answered John. Pontiac fixed him in his steady gaze, and for just an instant the gulf that lay between them was not so wide. Then Pontiac turned away to his affairs.

This time they struck out on the trail on their own. Oyan and his warriors would remain for the council and then move on with the great party of Natives to Detroit. It would be two hard days of travel back to the river where Pierre's canoe was hidden.

They walked as quickly as Samuel could manage. Away from the Odawa camp and the need to behave himself and be quiet, the little boy was again chattering endlessly. No one said anything to him in hopes that he would tire himself out. Only Dog seemed to listen. Since Samuel never required answers, John was free to think other thoughts.

He watched Marie and Pierre. There was no particular difference in their behavior toward each other. A few times John thought he saw their hands brush. He might have felt envy, but he did not. He liked both these people and only wished them well. Friendship it would be then; he would treasure them both.

That night when they camped, and Marie had taken Samuel to wash his face and hands after their dinner of rabbit, Pierre spoke to John.

"I thank you, John MacNeil, for speaking for me last night. You could have said something else, but you did not." Pierre knew how things might have gone had John's words been different.

"I said what I believed to be true. That is all. I would do no less for a friend," answered John honestly and Pierre nodded.

They watched Marie lead Samuel back, his head drenched from the scrub she had given him. It would be quite a life if they married, if she would truly have him as her husband, Pierre mused. Time would tell. He was young and brave and strong; he had his apple orchards and his house. All would be well no matter what the future might bring.

The next day they pressed on to the river. The wind had shifted yet again and was now coming from the east. John knew it would be blowing down the river toward

Detroit. An east wind almost always meant that foul weather was coming and he hoped they would reach the canoe and the fort before it hit. Then, while they were some distance from the water, they heard a sound ahead. Something huge was crashing through the bushes.

"It must be a bear or a moose," whispered Samuel nervously, squinting at the foliage and listening to the grunting snorts. "Nothing else could make such sounds!" Then the branches were parted and the creature stepped out.

"I have found them, Father!" bellowed Sean Doig over his shoulder. He turned to John and clasped the boy in his big arms. "And a sight for sore eyes you all are, especially you, John MacNeil. We were certain you were gone into the sky in the storm or, worse, to the bottom of the river!" Other bodies emerged from the brush. Natka stood back smiling, while Wallace and Alex thumped John on his back and shoulders. John realized that the big Scot's eyes were damp.

"I would never have forgiven myself," he sighed. "I thought you were gone forever, lad."

"I am tougher than that, Wallace," answered John, and his throat felt tight.

"'Tis true you are, lad," said Wallace. "None of us saw you go over, so quickly it all happened. One moment you were there, and the next you were not. In the storm we couldna turn the boat 'til we were at the fort. Your father sent us back to look for you."

"We searched the island and then the shore across from it. Your moccasins left a trail I knew well," said

Natka, and he hugged John to his chest. "It is good to see you are safe." John thought of Pontiac's words and of his anger. Surely life here among these people could be more than that?

"I am well, friend," he said quietly, stepping back and clasping Natka's shoulders. "It is good to see your face again."

"I am happy to see you even though we have not met," piped up Samuel and they laughed. John took on the introductions. Pierre, Wallace, and Natka had met. Alex and Sean bowed to Marie, and smiled greetings to Samuel. When the child learned who Wallace was, he wiggled in his excitement.

"Yes, Samuel," said John as they all started out again. "It is *that* Wallace, the one who owns the *Swift*. I trust you have sailed up the river in your fine bateau, sir? If you came in canoes, we will have a time dealing with Samuel."

"Indeed, lad. She waits for us all with wee Hamish standing watch on her. Are you a sailor, lad?"

"I would like to be," answered Samuel. "Will we sail to the fort?"

"That we will, lad," promised Wallace. Alex carried Samuel so that they would make better time, and in a few hours they broke out of the trees and onto the beach. They had emerged from the woods only a short distance from where Pierre's canoe had been left. It was safe and dry. All sign of the Odawas and their canoes had disappeared. Anchored in deeper water offshore, pulling hard on her anchor, the *Swift* pointed upstream. Hamish waved in delight.

"We will paddle out in the canoe. You can take it on board, I trust?" Pierre asked Wallace, who nodded.

"That'll be grand. We got a good soaking coming ashore this morning. Your canoe we will lash onto the deck. A simple matter."

In minutes they were all aboard the *Swift*. The wee lads brought the canoe up on the deck and tied it with line to the mast. Then they made ready to set sail. John breathed in the clean, sweet air and reveled at the feel of the boat under his feet once again. He watched the familiar drill as the anchor was hauled up and the mainsail and jib quickly raised. Wallace pulled hard on the tiller and turned the boat downstream. The sails billowed out on each side of the mast as the strong breeze filled them. Carried by the wind and the powerful current, they raced down the river.

"It looks like a bird, like the wings of a bird!" exclaimed Samuel. It was the first thing he had said since stepping aboard the *Swift*. Maybe Marie's father should build a boat, thought John. It might keep Samuel quiet.

It was a wonderful sail. The stiff breeze had raised small waves on the river's surface that slapped and splashed against the *Swift*. The sun shone warmly and only the rushing of the hull could be heard as it hissed over the water. The wee lads let the sails out and drew them in again, studying the canvas and judging what must be done for the most speed. Under Wallace's expert hand, the boat skimmed along. Hamish went forward and dug out baskets of food. There were cheeses and fresh bannock, a ripe melon, some cold meat, and boiled eggs.

"We never sail without proper provisions," he explained seriously. "A sailor must have plenty of food."

"Would you like to try steering, lad?" Wallace asked Samuel as they all ate. The child nodded. Wallace set his hand on the tiller, but did not remove his own. "If it were night you would pick a star to sail by." And John was transported back to more than a year ago when he first set his hands on the wheel of the *Amazon* as it left England.

"She almost feels alive, does she not?" he asked Samuel, and the boy simply nodded. Yes, John thought, Samuel's father must build a boat.

The wind blew fiercely and the lowering sun shone through the spread sails as they hurtled down the river. In a matter of hours they neared the fort. Even at a distance John could see the crowd that waited for them at the water gate and at the edge of the river. Just before they drew abreast of the fort, a single cannon blast welcomed them back.

Wallace leaned hard against the tiller and steered the *Swift* up into the wind so Hamish and Alex could drop the sails. At the same time, Sean lowered the anchor into the river's depths and the boat swung around. It turned broadside to the current for a moment, then the anchor bit into the bottom and the boat jerked. Alex and Hamish carefully folded and stowed the jib and mainsail while Sean cleared away what remained of their meal. Pierre's canoe was untied and dropped into the water. They all crowded into it and went ashore.

John could see his father standing there. His face was stony. His eyes gave away nothing of what he might be thinking. It had not occurred to John until now that Lord MacNeil might be angry with him. After all, it had meant that a search party had been sent out. Far more important events than his misadventure were happening in the fort. It must have been a mere nuisance.

John walked up to his father, his heart beginning to pound, his hands suddenly damp. He stopped in front of him. "Father, sir," he began carefully, but before John could go on, Lord MacNeil crushed him to his chest. He said nothing to his son for a moment, then stepped back. This boy. How dear John was to him. How could he ever have thought anything else back in England?

"I have returned, sir," said John. How hard it was to speak aloud. He could read his father's face and he realized that they were both feeling the same thing. More had happened between them this last year than a mere voyage. More than an ocean had been crossed.

Lord MacNeil cleared his throat before speaking, and blinked his eyes very hard several times. "Indeed you have, John. And with quite a party it seems. Doig, you, your sons, and Natka have my gratitude. LaButte, why am I not surprised to see you? You do turn up in the strangest places." Pierre smiled.

"Well, if I do not look for trouble she looks for me, monsieur," he said in explanation.

A large man pushed by Lord MacNeil. A woman followed him.

"Marie! Samuel! By all the saints, you are all in one piece, you both. I am too happy for the words! I can barely speak!" cried their father. He picked up Samuel and hugged him.

"Ah, my girl," said Marguerite as she brushed her daughter's hair back from her brow.

"*Ma mère*, do not say it. I know that if we had not been there, the whirlwind would not have caught us, and you would not have spent all these days in worry. But we are well. We are safe. John MacNeil and Pierre came to our rescue."

"I thought only to say how happy I am that you have come home," said her mother simply. Pierre was it? Until now they had been Monsieur LaButte and Mademoiselle Roy. Just what *had* happened out there? Ah, well. She was a young woman now. Perhaps a grandchild was not so many years away, after all?

Everyone moved into the fort. The chattering and laughter carried up and down Detroit's streets. Lemony light shone from the windows and somewhere a fiddle and a fife played. It was Sunday evening and the inevitable dance had begun at Captain Campbell's house. The wee lads disappeared to enjoy the evening's festivities but Wallace and Natka said their good nights. They had been in a few drawing rooms now and again. John knew that velvets and lace, the ceaseless whining of violins, and chattering ladies with sweeping skirts and carefully dressed hair were not for them.

As they walked, John and Marie tried to explain what had happened. Everyone was talking at the same time, and naturally, Samuel was carrying on with his own incredible version of the story. The storm, their capture of sorts, Pontiac. At that name, Lord MacNeil started.

"You were in an encampment with Pontiac?" he asked slowly. "And you were released unharmed."

"Indeed, Father. It was a little more complicated than that, but we were treated well. I have a message from Pontiac for King George."

"Of course. Why did I not guess?" He stared at his son. John was taller now than a year ago, full of confidence and the joy of what he did. He had been right to insist that John come along. Canada had done this to him.

"Well then, let us go to the house. Monsieur Roy, you and your family have accommodations for the night?"

"*Oui*, we do, thank you, monsieur. And you, Pierre, will come with us, *mon ami*."

"We shall clean you up a bit and join Captain Campbell and the new officers at Campbell's quarters, then, John. LaButte, for whatever role you played in this, I thank you." Pierre bowed as elegantly as any French lord.

"It was my pleasure, monsieur."

"Come with us, Pierre," insisted Margeurite. "You must tell us everything."

"Everything, madame?" he asked mischievously, not daring to look at Marie.

"Oh yes! It is most exciting," offered Samuel. "There will be a wedding and we went on the bateau — did you see it? I sailed it myself!" John could hear Samuel's ravings as he and his family and Pierre turned a corner and disappeared into the darkness.

John and his father entered the house in which they lived. It had seemed so cozy and comfortable only a few days ago. Now its walls closed in around John. He went up to his small room to change from what he suddenly realized was filthy clothing. He peeled off his borrowed shirt and, pouring water into a wash basin, splashed some onto his face and torso. No one would really notice him anyway. He pulled the tie from his tangled hair, tugged at the snarls with a wooden comb, and retied it back with a bow at the nape of his neck. Fresh breeches, a clean shirt and woven belt, his moccasins, and he was ready. Somehow a waistcoat and buckled shoes would not have felt correct.

He hurried down the steps and followed his father out into the street. Candlelight spilled from the windows of many houses. Others were in shadowy darkness. On a warm night such as this, many people sat outside enjoying the cool evening breezes. It was September now. John knew that autumn came quickly in this country and the winter was sure to be hard. What surprises would it bring?

Captain Campbell's home was ahead. The windows and doors were open and a glow from many candles lit the street in squares and rectangles of yellow. Laughter drifted in the air and figures appeared and disappeared as they moved through the room in a dance. A violin played a lively tune.

John and his father entered the commander's house.

The music did not stop and people barely looked their way, so intent were they upon each other and the evening's entertainment. It was only when Captain Campbell saw them and strode over that heads turned their way.

"I heard!" he cried, shaking John's hand briskly. "It was a terrible storm, my boy. What luck that Doig and the Odawa found you."

"There is more to it than that, sir." He must share this with Campbell. In the unreal setting of this house, far from the wild heart of the forest, Pontiac's warning dropped into his mind like a cold lump of ice. "There were four of us on the island as it happened, Pierre LaButte and the children of Pierre Roy. In trying to reach Detroit in LaButte's canoe, we were taken by a party of Pontiac's men." Lord MacNeil stood in silence. Did John understand just how fortunate they were to be back here?

"So you say?" questioned a deep voice. A scarlet-uniformed officer had crossed the room and now stood near them. Lieutenant Lindsay, a goblet in his hand, was just behind the stranger.

"Major Gladwin, sir, Captain Lord James MacNeil. Captain MacNeil, Major Henry Gladwin, the new commander of Fort Detroit." The officers bowed to each other solemnly.

"Welcome, sir," said Lord MacNeil. "You have arrived at quite a time. It is usually quiet in this place."

"I dare say, MacNeil. Did I hear the name Pontiac spoken? You have seen him, boy?" Locals! The Major sighed to himself. Here he was shortly arrived at the fort and feeling none too well at that, and now a mere boy tries to start a most distressing rumor.

"This is my son, John MacNeil, sir," said Lord MacNeil to Gladwin. "There was a storm. He and others were lost, and it seems they spent time in an encampment upriver with the Odawas."

"It would have been quite safe," Lindsay threw in casually as he sipped his Madeira. "These people are content enough with what we give them."

"I agree," nodded Gladwin, wiping his brow. "They want peace with their English brothers, as they put it. Life with us may not be as easy as it was with the French. No more concessions are to be made — General Amherst is clear on that point — but they will live without them." And Gladwin turned away from John.

A woman's laugh rang out across the room. John paused, the music and chatter suspended around him like baubles on silver chains. He could let it pass and remain a quiet and untried youth. Or he could speak out and leave behind forever that English boy who passed like a strange creature among the people here. He made his choice. With a few simple words he planted his heart and soul in the soil of Canada.

"I think not, sir." Both Major Gladwin's and Lieutenant Lindsay's heads tipped back a bit, and they looked down their noses at John. Is there a part of military training where they teach them to do that? John wondered. If the matter had not been so deadly serious he might have laughed aloud.

"What did you say?" purred Gladwin slowly.

"I said, I think not," answered John at the same silky, courtly speed. "You have no idea the mettle of these people, Major Gladwin. They are not content and I do not think peace can last."

"You cannot be certain of such things, John," said Lord MacNeil, and yet he knew what his son said must be true. John smiled at his father and spoke more loudly now. Eyes turned his way and conversations near them dropped off as people listened.

"Oh, I am quite certain, Father," John said with a confidence he had not heard before in his own voice. Then he turned his unwavering, gray eyes on Gladwin. "We were there, after all, sir. I saw the weapons and the war paint. I spoke with Pontiac at his fire. This was their place long before we came here, and in spite of what policies General Amherst may decree, that does count for something. They will not bend — and why should they or anyone else who lives here?"

"The rigors of his captivity," whispered Lindsay theatrically. "Shock, perhaps? The boy needs a rest." John dismissed Lindsay's wigged presence with a cold glance.

"Do not be ridiculous, Lindsay," said Campbell shortly. "This is serious. Rumors fly everywhere. If there is war because of a policy handed down from New York, you shall see what the term *shock* means." The room had grown far too quiet. Almost everyone listened now, and even some of the dancers had stopped.

Enough of this, thought Gladwin, and with a measuring look at this odd son of MacNeil's, he clapped his hands sharply.

"Is this a party or a wake, Campbell? A brisk piece of music, fiddler!" But the fiddler played only a few bars of the tune. The music trailed off as its last notes echoed in the air. The gathering became deathly silent except for the footsteps of a solitary man. The crowd parted for Pierre LaButte, who walked slowly across the room.

"Who ordered it done?" said Pierre softly to Campbell. Gladwin stared at the interpreter, dirty, unshaven, his clothing travel-stained. A dangerous heat burned in his blue eyes.

"Who ordered what done, LaButte?" asked Campbell in confusion. He liked this man, but he did not like what he saw at the moment.

"The trees. My orchard outside the fort here. Who ordered it cut?" John caught his breath. He knew how much the trees meant to Pierre, how he must have cared for each one, treasuring the fruit they bore.

"I ordered the trees cut," spoke up Major Gladwin smartly. "They were dangerous to the safety of this fort." His head hurt and these people were truly beginning to grate on his nerves.

"Dangerous!" shouted LaButte, stepping forward, and John reached out his hand and held onto the trembling length of his friend's arm. "They were *trees*. Do the English make war on apple orchards now?"

"The line of vision, man," said Campbell calmly. "Major Gladwin felt that if we ever do come under attack, the trees would have been perfect cover for approaching enemies." John felt the muscles in Pierre's arms bunch and tense.

"The enemy? I am not so certain these days that the enemy is outside Detroit." And shrugging off John's hand, he turned and left the room. John glanced over at his father, then followed Pierre out into the night.

He ran down the street and past the parade ground. Ahead of him, he saw Pierre exit the fort through the east gate. John trailed after him into the cool air beyond the walls. The garden stood some distance away. There was the gardener's building in which LaButte had sometimes lived. The rows of cabbages and herbs were untouched, but beyond them where apples trees had stood, their branches heavy with fruit, there was only a tumble of trunks and branches. Some of the trees had been chopped into firewood. Branches had been burned. The fruit lay on the ground, trampled. A rich scent of apples rose in the night air.

"They did not even think to pick the apples," said Pierre in a stunned voice to Marie, who stood there. Silvery lines of tears shone on her cheeks. "What a waste."

"You can replant them," said Marie. She stooped and picked up a small undamaged apple. "I will save the seeds for you. We can do this!"

"I will help you as well, Pierre," offered John. Pierre took the apple from Marie and wiped it on his sleeve. He took a bite from it and passed it to her. She bit deeply into the fruit and passed it to John. He took the last bite. It was a bittersweet taste, the tang of fall and things coming to an end. He gave the core to Marie who slipped it into a fold of her skirt.

"Will you stay here?" John asked him, and he flinched at Pierre's jaded smile.

"I will stay in Detroit. It is my home. I have the house on Ste. Anne's Street, as small as it is."

"Surely you will not translate for Gladwin," said Marie, who had already heard about the fort's new commander. She was gathering apples and holding them in her skirt.

"I must, Marie," Pierre said. "I can do nothing else. Perhaps I can keep the worst from happening. I will translate for Gladwin only because there are too many good people living in this place to leave their fates entirely to the fools who have come here." He looked sideways at John. "Excepting a fine fellow such as you, John MacNeil."

John smiled sadly at his friend and the three of them started back to the fort. A few apples tumbled from Marie's skirt. He ran back and picked them up. The sentry who watched them enter the gate shook his head at such foolishness. The boy had missed an apple. The soldier kicked at it and the bits of fruit exploded into the night. Apple trees. All this fuss and bother about apple trees!

# CHAPTER
# SIXTEEN

Several days later a second great council was held at
Fort Detroit, and hundreds of Hurons, Potawatomis,
Senecas, Odawas, and other tribes were in attendance.
John saw Pontiac at a distance, surrounded by his
warriors. They nodded to each other but did not speak.
Sir William Johnson, the Native agent who had also
come for the council, worked hard to smooth the waters,
in spite of the fact that the British had built yet more
trading posts without the permission of the tribes. His
gifts to them and the huge feast held in their honor were
in defiance of General Amherst's policies. John would
always remember Johnson as a wise man. Lieutenant
Lindsay saw it otherwise.

"I will be glad to be rid of this place," he told John. "I
leave for Fort Michilimackinac next week. It requires
a firm hand as well, it seems. All the best, MacNeil.
You will need it if Campbell and now Gladwin continue
this nonsense."

After that, a peaceful, early fall arrived. Maple trees
turned as scarlet as the coats of King George's army.

Oaks and birches glowed the color of burnished brass buttons. Then a hard wind from the north blew for days. The leaves began to fall, and bare black branches poked at the sky.

John saw his friends only a few times in the next months. Still bitter, Pierre found one excuse after another to be absent from the fort. Marie and Samuel settled back into the calm life they led with their parents. John found himself alone much of the time; he could barely believe that existence here could suddenly be so uneventful. Before winter came, Wallace, Natka, and the wee lads would safely ground and anchor the *Swift* in a nearby shallow river that ran into the Detroit River. There she would be sheltered from any dangerous winter ice. They themselves would go north to hunt and trap for a month or so.

John turned back to his letters and drawings. In truth, it was a relief to be able to once more write to his sister, losing himself in the thoughts he penned for her. The portrait of Pontiac had been sent off almost at once with a letter for the King's eyes only. But the Court in England was a world away, and he could not be certain that his words would mean anything.

*It was a strange thing,* he wrote to Jane. *I have always been raised to think that we must make the world all England. Yet when I spoke with Pontiac and saw this place through his eyes, what I once believed now seems to me to be foolishness. We will live here, yes, the thing has gone too far to change now. But it seems to me that we should be able to live side by side in peace.*

*There are wonderful people on the frontier, Jane. You can see that by my drawings. A few especially, you would truly like. If you ever come here, and I cannot see why you would not do so, I believe you will find a friend in Marie Roy. She could not be more different than you if it were planned. Yet she sees life in the same way. She wants the same things as you do — in her heart she could be your sister.*

John told her everything about Marie and Samuel and Pierre. He took nearly a week to finish his letter. But when he had, they, as well as Wallace and Natka and the three wee lads, had come to life for Jane on the paper. The letter went out in the morning with other dispatches and he ached with a slight sense of loss. He wandered the fort for several days, not feeling the desire to draw or write. He knew the long winter that lay ahead. Somehow the nearly bare trees now depressed him.

Then, an invitation came. It was not to one of the dances that Captain Campbell held each week. It was not for a dinner party at one of the finer homes of the fort. It came directly from the lips of Marie Roy herself. John had been happily surprised to find her standing at their door one clear, fall afternoon. Her father was there at the fort on business, and she and Samuel had joined him. Samuel was with her father now, no doubt making business impossible.

She was lovelier than ever, thought John. What a fine couple she and Pierre would make if they were to marry.

Her hair hung in a single braid down her back. Silky strands had come loose. They blew about her face in the cool wind that skittered between the houses. Her cheeks were glowing and her green eyes smiled happily. She had draped a blanket over her shoulders against the fall weather. Its striped fabric flapped in the wind.

"Marie!" he said warmly.

"John, you are well?" she asked in a soft voice that held a hint of shyness.

"I am. And you?" Where was the easy banter of a month ago? he wondered. "Please, come in." But she put up her hand and shook her head.

"I cannot. Père wishes to leave. Samuel is making him half crazy. Will you come to the house this Saturday evening for a meal? You did say you would finish the drawing." He knew of their cabin that lay on the banks of the river not so far from the fort.

"Yes, I will be there. How good it will be to spend time with you again." I cannot believe I just said that, he groaned to himself. She smiled and waved, then turned and walked away. John was sure he could hear Samuel's high-pitched complaints in the distance as Marie sought out her father and brother.

The next Saturday he chose his clothing with care, bathing with warmed water in a large basin and even washing his hair. His father watched with amusement as John rushed down the steps, ready for his outing, but he dared not even smile.

"How do I look?" he asked Lord MacNeil. John had put on a full-sleeved shirt and clean, wool britches with high, heavy moccasins. He shrugged into a coat, for the evening was cool. His long hair was tied back with a beaded thong. The document case was draped over his shoulder, and his eyes were bright with excitement. He looks like someone who had never set foot in England, Lord MacNeil realized. John had become a part of this country in this short time in a way he himself never would.

"Well, it would hardly pass muster with General Amherst, but you look impressive," observed Lord MacNeil gruffly. To have said anything else would have been cruel. I must be getting old, he thought, shaking his head.

John walked briskly through the fort. There were fewer people coming to trade now; many had gone north for the fall and winter hunts. Still, the streets were busy with soldiers, militia, and French civilians all upon some mission. John left through the east gate. He did not look at the garden or the stumps of apple trees. He continued along the path that ran near the river. Red light from the sun setting behind him glinted on the river's surface, and the season's last crickets chirped weakly from the tall brown grass.

He smelled smoke from the Roy homestead before he saw the cabin. That, and the deep barking of Dog, led him straight to them. Pierre Roy stepped into the doorway with a musket in his hand — one could not be too careful these days. John called out a greeting.

"It is I, Monsieur Roy! John MacNeil!"

"Welcome!" Roy called back. A small shape pushed

into the doorway and Samuel was backlit by the light and lamps that shone from within. Recognizing their guest, he burst out and ran across the yard to John.

"Where have you been, John?" he asked happily as he wrapped his arms around his friend.

"I may ask the same thing," answered John, hugging the boy. Roy gestured for them to enter. Inside the house it was warm and pleasantly full of the smells of cooking food. Marie turned from the meat she was basting as Margeurite Roy entered the room, wiping her hands on a cloth.

"John! It is so good that you are here," said Marie fondly. How happy she looks, he thought.

"Welcome to our fire," added Margeurite.

"*Bonsoir*, John MacNeil," said LaButte, and John turned in surprise. Pierre sat in the shadows where he had been watching them all.

"I though perhaps you had gone north to trap," said John. Pierre pulled his chair to the fire and the men sat knee to knee while Marie and her mother worked.

"Not this year, *mon ami*," said Pierre, and he looked over at Marie. "This year is different."

"How?" John asked, although he somehow knew what the answer would be.

"Tonight is a celebration, John MacNeil, one we wished to share with you."

"Oh?" said John. "A birthday? A special feast?"

"No!" shrieked Samuel. "A wedding! It will be wonderful, at the Miami village in the spring. We will all go and you must come too! You must bring Wallace and Natka and the wee lads." It was as John thought.

"It is true," Marie's father said happily. "The banns, the first ones, they will be read at Ste. Anne's tomorrow morning at the mass. They have sense, these two, and they will wait until May. It will be at the village of Marguerite's people, as it should be. You must be there to rejoice with us, John."

"Of course I will be there. How could I miss it?" said John to Marie and Pierre, and although he felt happiness for his friends, a soft wing of regret brushed his heart.

"*Bien*! Bring wine, Margeurite, and we will toast the happy couple," said Roy.

His wife and Marie did just that. It was the sweet red wine that Roy made himself. Even Samuel was allowed a small, very watered portion. They toasted Marie and Pierre, and John thought he had never seen two happier-looking people.

It was a long, joyful evening filled with laughter and far too much food. They told stories of the summer's adventures and Samuel entertained them all by making Dog beg and roll over for bits of meat. Marie's father got out his fiddle and they danced until they collapsed, laughing and sweaty, in the chairs by the fire. At last, worn out with the celebration, John said he must leave.

"I will walk home with you, John MacNeil," offered Pierre, taking up his musket. "Major Gladwin swears we are all as safe as infants in cradleboards, but I am not so sure." He bowed to Marie. There would be no kisses until the marriage day as far as Margeurite Roy was concerned. John said his goodbyes. Then they went into the darkness that lay between the cabin and Fort Detroit.

"Wait!" called Marie and she rushed out after them without even a shawl.

"What is it, *ma petite*? I know you cannot bear to have me out of your sight for a moment, but is this not extreme?" Marie shook her head hopelessly at this silliness, and she turned to John.

"The drawing. You did not finish it." John looked down at the document case that he carried. He had not opened it or even thought of the sketch that curled inside it all evening.

"How can this be, John MacNeil? Since when are you so forgetful?" asked Pierre with feigned suspicion, but he only laughed. Marie was safely promised to him.

"Well, it shall have to be another time, then," said John, and Pierre slapped him across the shoulders.

"Another time then!" said Pierre and his happy laughter danced into the might.

But there was no other time. In a week the first heavy snow fell, and Detroit was locked in winter's icy grip.

# CHAPTER
# SEVENTEEN

It was a harder winter than anyone could remember for years. At first, thick clouds of steam rose over the Detroit River. In February, the quickly flowing waters froze, and for a while it was possible to walk across to the opposite shore. Storms and deep cold seized the fort and the settlements around it. Weeks before, they had begun to cut back on rations. Soldiers went out to hunt, but found that the tribes whose villages surrounded the fort were doing the same thing. Game was difficult to find, and every scrap of a deer or rabbit was eaten. The icy days with their slate skies and the long, chilling nights brought hardship for everyone.

Wallace, Natka, and the wee lads returned just before the harshest weather was upon them. In spite of their layers of heavy clothing — thick boots, wool breeches, and hooded coats — they all were half frozen. They stood before the fire in Lord MacNeil's house thawing themselves and gave him news that he would pass on to his superiors. The wee lads shook snow and ice from their long, black braids.

"You wouldna want to spend your winter in the bush this year, my friends," said Wallace, rubbing his hands to ease the pain of the frostbite that had nipped them.

"'Twas the wee, woolly caterpillars, Father," said Sean. "The black and brown ones. I told you they were woollier than ever, and that is the sign of a hard winter."

"Nay, 'twas the pine cones. The trees were heavy with pine cones. That is the sign of a hard winter," insisted Hamish, and Alex nodded solemnly in agreement.

"It wasna just the weather — caterpillars, and pine cones considered, lads. I think you wouldna find a welcome at any village at which you might try to shelter."

"There is so much bad feeling then?" asked MacNeil as he poured hot drinks all around. The men warmed their hands on the steaming mugs.

"No powder. No balls or shot, no muskets, they cannot hunt," said Natka, rubbing his palms over his face. John thought the Odawa looked thin and tired. Lord MacNeil shook his head. What would happen here?

"We willna starve, never fear. There is game and fish, if you ken how to find them." They did not go hungry, but it was a long winter nonetheless.

John had little to do except sketch and write. It would be a lengthy letter this time, Jane, he thought. It will take me all winter to write it. Before the hard weather had set in, only one last dispatch and packet of letters had made it to Fort Detroit. Other than word of mouth and the occasional foolhardy traveler, they had to wait until spring for news from away. Few people came to the fort.

He saw LaButte once or twice, but Marie nested in her parents' cozy house up the river.

"She wishes to be with her family for these next months," Pierre explained to John. "After that, her life will be with me. She sends her friendship, John MacNeil, of that you may be sure." John knew in his heart this was true.

A letter from Jane had arrived in that last packet delivered to the fort. It had been filled with news. It rambled on about all the small details of her life, going from one topic to another exactly as she would have done had they been together. He read it, and in fact, all of her letters again and again by candle and firelight through the long, still afternoons. He could nearly feel her there with him as the words she had written echoed in his mind.

*My dear John,* she wrote this latest time. *All are well here. Baby Jamie sends his love. At least, I do believe that is what he means. It sounds somewhat like a small belch, I suppose, but I prefer to think he is talking to us.*

*Mary is often tired. She is two hundred years old, I think, John. She was Mama's nurse before she was mine. I hope she will be here for my children. Not that I will have any soon. Henry and I have decided to wait to marry until you and Father return. Father may have been difficult and distant in years past, but I do owe him this, and how could I marry without you here? Wait we will, and until then, we range up and down the countryside collecting plants and unusual flowers. I have found that I have a talent for sketching them where I failed at drawing people.*

*I would like to travel farther. Henry says that when we are wed we will have a ship. I will prefer that to his family home, which is enormous and drafty and has far too many rooms. We will journey to distant lands together. How amazing that will be. And to think that once I spoke of marrying a pirate!*

*Somehow I received a letter from you just last week, although it must have been sent late in the year. None have ever come so quickly. Is the delivery of the King's mail improving? Think of how quickly letters will arrive in two hundred years!*

*Marie. I do believe I like her, even though we have not met. And you think she will marry this dashing fellow, Pierre? How exciting. If it happens, please give them a gift on my behalf. You are so clever. I know that you will think of something.*

*On the topic of gifts and weddings, King George was wedded to Princess Charlotte in September. It was an amazing spectacle. Henry and I plan a far more simple event, something that does not involve a cathedral and guests all eating during the ceremony. Lord Elgie was there. You would not have been disappointed in his performance: pheasant soup right in his lap!*

Jane. How he missed her and, he supposed, all of Brierly. It was only in these quiet times that he allowed himself to dwell on these feelings. How he longed to see her once again. And the baby brother he had never held in his arms, and dear old Mary and David and Mama, no matter how aloof she might try to be. And, of course, Lord Elgie with his food-spattered waistcoat.

"What a thing it would be to see Lord Elgie and the wee lads at the same table," said John aloud. That image was hardly for the faint of heart.

And so the winter passed with its long nights and late sunrises. One early morning when he stepped outside the house at his usual hour, his feet squeaking in the snow, his breath freezing the hairs in his nostrils, John realized that he could see a pink tinge in the sky. The sun was peeking out beyond the forest. Each day after that it rose a little earlier. Snow began to melt and drip. The Natives and the people at the fort made maple sugar and they all ate it on lumps of clean, white snow.

Ice broke up on the river and lake and drifted past the fort in high floes. In April, Wallace's sons went up to check on the *Swift*. She had wintered well, it was reported. "And that is good, lad," Wallace observed, "for we shall need her to sail to the wedding."

The wedding! Had the spring passed so quickly? Was it May already, and were those lilacs and dandelions blooming along the water? John supposed they were.

One morning in May, the *Swift* waited for them in the river at the water gate. The lads had scrubbed her decks and rails. The sails were ready for hoisting. They would sail down the river and be at the Miami village in no time with this good wind. John's father saw them off.

They all wore their best. In fact, each item John wore

was new, since he had grown during the winter. His legs were longer and his shoulders had strained the cloth of his old shirts. Today he wore a wool coat atop his heavy linen shirt and fine leggings rose above his high, beaded moccasins.

"If you ever return to England, and I stress the if, for one does not know how long one shall be here, you must do something with your wardrobe," said Lord MacNeil in exasperation. What a sight the boy was!

"Why?" asked John. Why indeed, thought his father. Why indeed?

At last they were all assembled, an amazing spectacle, to be sure. Natka's head was freshly shaved with the clam shell he so expertly wielded. His face was carefully painted. Wallace wore his best kilt and a gigantic sporran of wolf skin. The wee lads had even combed their hair. The crew of the *Swift* set off down the river.

When they reached the village, cries and cheers greeted them from the sandy beach. Smoke from cook fires drifted in the wind and at the shore, children waded in the cold water, their teeth chattering. Canoes came out to the anchored boat to ferry them to shore. A boy waited there for them.

"Samuel?" asked John in surprise. Could this be the little boy he had carried to Pontiac's camp? Samuel had grown during these last months, and he no longer leaned his head back quite so far to look up at John. Dog scampered around them all, barking and panting joyfully, his brushy tail beating a happy rhythm.

"Yes, it is me — who else would they send? We have been waiting all morning only for you, you know. She said she could not be married unless her friend was here!" On and on he went as they hiked up to the village. He may be taller now, but he is still Samuel, thought John.

He saw Marie before she saw him. There was a calmness and poise about her that he had not noticed before. What she wore for her wedding day was a mixture of each world that had shaped her life, touches of both French and Miami. Her sleekly braided hair was dressed with beads, ribbons, and feathers. The perfect part that ran down the center of her head was painted with a delicate line of vermilion. She wore a silk bodice and a skirt of fine cloth with shining satiny ribbons running along the hem. Silver earrings dangled from her earlobes. The wampum belt that draped across one shoulder was tied at her waist. It had been carefully made of white shell beads, with blue dragonflies worked down its length. She turned suddenly and caught sight of John. Her warm smile shone out at him.

"They are here, Pierre!" she called to the man she was to marry. Pierre stepped out from the simple church and they both walked to meet their guests.

"Welcome, *mes amis*," said Pierre warmly as he clasped John's hand and then the hands of the others. In a clean white shirt, leggings of soft, dark green wool, and a new ribbon in his hair, he was an elegant bridegroom. He put his arm around Marie's shoulder. "Come inside. Père Renard grows impatient."

A small group was gathered in the building. Leaving Dog to lie in the sunshine outside, Samuel went to his parents. Other men and women stood behind them. Candles glowed on the altar and there was a soft murmuring as people watched the bride and groom enter the church behind the new arrivals.

"John MacNeil," said Pierre as John prepared to take his place with the others. "A ceremony such as this requires two witnesses. Marie has asked her cousin, Rose Ouabankikove, to stand for her. I will choose my own witness. At least I hope you will be my witness. Will you, John?" asked Pierre. John swallowed and then smiled into his friend's eyes.

"Of course I shall. I would be honored." And he walked slowly to the altar rail with Marie and Pierre and the plump, smiling Rose. There Père Renard took the couple's marriage contract from Pierre Roy. The priest read it over and, nodding his approval, handed it back to Marie's father. Père Renard walked to the altar rail and addressed the congregation in French.

"Marriage is a very old and holy sacrament and not to be taken lightly. It will bind you together for life, my children," he said gently. And so began the solemn French service that would join Marie and Pierre in marriage. Each of them, first Pierre, then Marie, said their vows to the other. Pierre's voice sounded strong and certain. Then Marie repeated the words the priest said to her.

"I marry and take you for my husband, Pierre. I swear that I shall be your faithful wife. I will care for you in all your needs for as long as God chooses to leave us together." John listened as she swore to be a loving and faithful wife to Pierre.

"I will bless the ring now, Monsieur LaButte, and you may then place it upon the finger of your bride," said Père Renard. Pierre's face paled.

"Ah, yes. There is the matter of the ring, mon Père," said Pierre, realizing that he had forgotten it. He looked around himself desperately as though the ring might suddenly appear. Marie sighed. No matter, it would not mean they were any less married.

"Well then we will proceed without the ring," said Père Renard kindly. It was not the first time a nervous and eager bridegroom had forgotten the ring. John looked down at Jane's Pea Ring on his finger. He thought of what she had said nearly two years ago. Never take it off unless it is for the most important reason, she had cautioned him. What could be more important than this?

"I have a ring," said John. He pulled the Pea Ring from his finger and gave it to Pierre. The other man took the ring in shocked surprise.

"Oh, no, John. That is your sister's ring. It is too precious to you to give up like this," exclaimed Marie, her voice trembling.

"Take it, please. She wished me to make a gift to you at your wedding. This is the gift." Marie said nothing more. She only looked at John in the way a true friend looks at another. Père Renard blessed the ring, and Pierre slipped it on Marie's finger. The priest completed the marriage ceremony in Latin and pronounced them married.

They all signed the register. Marie and Rose, who could not write, made their marks beneath the names that Pierre wrote for them. John saw that for her name, Marie had drawn a small dragonfly. It was done.

"And now 'tis time for the wedding ceilidh," roared Wallace as they stepped out of the church. "It canna be a wedding without a party!"

It was a feast. There was baked squash, corn soup with duck, and newly baked gallette. Smoke from roasting venison and moose drifted in the air. Fish baked in the coals, and pots of raccoon and beaver stews bubbled over the fires. The Miamis were much taken with the wee lads and the amount of food they were consuming.

Later there was dancing. The haunting sounds of drums and the wavering voices of Miami singers mixed with tunes from Pierre Roy's fiddle. People danced around the fires, while old men and women sat wrapped in their blankets. Hours before the festivities were over, Pierre and Marie motioned to John and the three of them slipped away from the village into the night. They walked along the beach. Stars glittered above them and a fresh wind blew though the trees.

"We are here tonight, John MacNeil, but we leave in the morning for Pêche. The fort will be our home, but we will still spend time on the island. I must see to my orchard there, you know. Perhaps we will build a log house, a bigger camp."

"How will you get there?" asked John as they crunched through the sand. "You could sail back with us."

"You are kind, John, but we will use my canoe. It will be slower, but we have the time," answered Marie, taken yet again by his thoughtfulness.

"Your canoe? It was destroyed in the storm." He stopped and looked out onto the water.

"Pierre made one for me," she laughed. "It was a wedding gift."

"I told you that day of the great storm that she would have another canoe," reminded Pierre. "I meant what I said." And he smiled fondly at his wife.

"I have a gift for you as well," said John and he slipped the document case from his shoulder and pulled off its cap.

"You have given me a gift already," protested Marie as she watched him.

"That was from Jane. This is from me." And he gave her a heavy roll. She pulled the cord that tied it, and carefully unrolled the paper. Marie smiled.

"Look, Pierre, John has finished the portrait. And I did not even have to pose for him." She stared down at her image. He had completed it from memory.

"We will hang it proudly in our home, John MacNeil," promised Pierre. John took the portrait from Marie and carefully rolled it up again. He slipped it back into the case.

"I will keep it safe for you until we meet once more," he said. And before he could stop himself, he leaned forward, took her hands, and gently kissed her cheek. "A happy life to you, Marie, and to you, as well, Pierre.

I hope that when Jane marries, she and her Henry are as well matched as you two."

"*Au revoir*, John MacNeil!" called Pierre as he took Marie's hand and led her away. She turned once, and her sweet, joyful smile lit her face. Then she was gone. John never saw her again.

# CHAPTER
# EIGHTEEN

Samuel was dreadfully ill the next day, and his parents shook their heads over him. Wallace had invited Pierre and Margeurite to sail back to the fort on the *Swift*. There was plenty of room for their canoe. Normally Samuel would have been thrilled to sail back to Detroit on the *Swift*. Now, as the boat sailed up the river, he moaned endlessly and leaned over the side, retching miserably. Hiding his smiles, Hamish took on the task of clutching the back of Samuel's shirt as the boy hung across the boat's rails.

"He is making the worst noises," said John, not without sympathy. At each sound, Dog cocked his big head, first to one side and then to the other.

"You would too, if you had put into your belly what the lad did last night!" chuckled Wallace. "They all learn the hard way!" But Samuel was made of tougher stuff than anyone might have guessed and in time, thoroughly empty, he was able to sit up and somewhat enjoy the sail.

The Detroit River's ever-present current ran against them beneath the *Swift's* hull, but a steady southwest wind gusted from the stern, and they made good time. It seemed to John that the wedding, in spite of being an event that had changed two people's lives, had almost been a dream.

Once back at the fort, his life fell into its familiar, homely patterns. Spring grew into summer, and John once again roamed the countryside with Wallace and Natka. He sometimes saw Pierre, for the interpreter was called to Detroit many times to speak for Major Gladwin and the English. But he did not see Marie.

"She will have our child this winter," Pierre told him with great happiness in his voice. Marie preferred to stay close to the camp LaButte had improved upon at the island. The wigwam was larger now and more heavily reinforced. Later on, she would return to her mother's home for the birth of the child. Then, most certainly, Pierre's little family would live at the fort in his house on Ste. Anne's street.

"What wonderful news!" said John warmly. "She is well, I hope?"

"She is a stubborn one, my Marie," admitted Pierre, lifting his shoulders in resignation. "She feels strong and so wants to stay at Pêche Island. She is happiest there, she says. I do not worry. Samuel and her mother are with her, and these absences of mine are short. You must come and visit with us, my friend. We can laugh over the old times."

Yes he must, John agreed — he would do it soon. And yet for some reason, he did not. The bittersweet memories seemed to hold him back. There was always another unexplored cove to visit, a new face to sketch, or a secret place in the forest to which he might escape.

He wrote to Jane often. With the summer weather, couriers made good time and dispatches flew back and forth in the triangle that was Fort Detroit, the port of New York, and England. Before John was ready for the end of the long, sunny days, the air grew cool and fall had come. There were three hard frosts in a row. The maples blazed with color and John could see his breath when he walked about at night. Each dawn the grass crackled beneath his feet, and his steps left melted footprints on the sparkling whiteness. Steady north winds blew and stripped the leaves from the beeches and oaks, baring them and setting their branches waving against the sky. Winter settled upon Fort Detroit.

One February morning John walked down the hallway of their house, ready to set out on foot to draw the winter scenery. His father's voice stopped him.

"Come here, John," he called quietly to his son. John paused and entered the room where his father sat at his desk, papers spread before him.

"What is it, Father? Word from Mama? Is all well, sir?" He did not like the drawn look on his father's face. He had seen it more and more often as tensions increased between the English military and the tribes in the last months.

Lord MacNeil looked up at his son. There would be war in this place, a war more brutal and horrible than any could imagine. But his prayers had been answered: John would be spared the fighting. MacNeil would never have been able to send John home himself since the boy was, after all, the King's own artist. As unofficial as it might be, he had a duty to perform here. But word had come from the Crown itself, a late post sent many months before, and in an instant everything had changed.

"There is a letter here from His Majesty's secretary on behalf of King George. You are to return to England. It seems His Majesty would meet the artist who has made Canada come to life for him." He passed the letter to his son and John read the royal document. It was as his father had said. He would travel slowly overland to Albany, then on to New York. He would spend time drawing and recording new things for the King to see, but at the latest, he was to depart for England by summer of the new year, 1763.

"I cannot leave you here, Father," said John helplessly. "I know what is being said. There will be war. Pontiac will lead them. You need not shelter me since I am no longer a child. I know exactly what such a war will be like and I want to stand here with you when it happens." He drew himself up and looked at his father steadily. Only the apple wood popping in the fireplace broke the silence.

No, he is not a child, thought MacNeil. He is a man. If John had come to manhood in England, how different he might have been. MacNeil thought of David with his courtly manner and fine, cultured bearing. He looked at John who stood across from him, tousled and determined. At fifteen years of age he was more experienced than his oldest son David might ever be. How was it that he had never known how much like himself John really was? He sighed and cleared his throat.

"You must go. One cannot question such commands. I shall be fine," said Lord MacNeil briskly, striving for a light tone of voice. "This is a strong fort and we will do our best to keep peace here. No objections now. You will have provisions and warm clothing since it is no small thing to journey in winter. I shall give you enough money to purchase what you need as you go. I have word that the *Amazon* will be in New York by the spring. She will take you home to England." Lord MacNeil carried on as much to distract himself as his son from what must happen.

And so they planned it together over the next days, the first thing they had truly done alone together in this place and possibly the last. John would leave for Albany and then travel on to New York with Natka and Wallace. There would be no guard, no party of red-coated soldiers. It was safer that way, slipping through the deep forests and back ways in the wilderness.

"The wee lads'll return with the *Swift* to the Miami village of their mother," Wallace told John. "As her bairns, they are members of her tribe, you see. They will be safe, and my heart will rest easy 'til I see them once again."

They all left one morning before dawn, when heavy mist rolled over the river. A passing flock of jays called their strange, lonely sounds. Goodbyes had been said the day and night before. No one except Lord MacNeil and the sleepy watchmen saw them depart, leaving the fort in careful silence. Down at the water gate the wee lads were helping Wallace and Natka load the canoe. At the river's edge John turned and faced his father. Lord MacNeil let his eyes drift over his son. How young the boy suddenly looked.

"Bid farewell to Pierre and Marie LaButte for me, Father. It is my one regret that I cannot do it myself," said John. He peered up the river where Pêche Island lay shrouded in mist. Memories of the place and what had happened there flooded back in a sweet rush.

"I will, do not fear," said his father. "They are your good friends — they will understand." John nodded. They reached out their hands and squeezed each other's shoulders at the same moment.

"I will return here, Father. You know that, do you not?"

"I know it, John. This place has claimed you as its own, I am afraid." Lord MacNeil laughed, but in his heart he felt a small sadness. Wallace and Natka stood to one side, steadying the canoe in the cold water, their breath rising in faint ghostly puffs. John looked around one last time and set the image of Detroit in his mind. He turned his eyes for a silent moment to his father, then climbed into the canoe. MacNeil watched as it carried his son into the mist and disappeared.

John had never traveled in this manner. They went slowly, carefully, and he had much time to draw, although with his chilled hands, it was not easy. He would pull off his mittens with his teeth and crouch with drawing paper set across his lap. He sketched herds of deer, startled in the empty, leafless forests. Beneath his fingers, lines of late ducks and geese flew in wavering vees across the pictures.

They slowly backtracked along the icy waterways,

from Lake Erie to Lake Ontario, then inland following the Albany trade route. They avoided some Native villages and only stopped at homesteads where the people were familiar to Wallace or Natka. John felt a wary apprehension, which grew to be a part of him. Each snapping twig sent a message; each calling bird was considered and judged. Was the birdsong a real thing or a warning sent out from one enemy to another?

The days were cold and brisk and the travel was easy, since no winter storms rose. Still, the frosty nights were chilling; only the coals of small fires warmed them, but John learned to sleep rolled in his blanket with the hood of his heavy wool coat pulled over his head.

"I wonder just how much of an adventure you would think this is, Jane?" he often whispered to himself as he squirmed to get comfortable on the hard ground.

But no danger came to them and they reached Albany in safety before the first light flakes of snow drifted from a still, gray sky. Wallace knew a jolly widow who kept a tavern in the busiest part of town. How strange it was to sleep in a bed above the noise and carryings on of the common room. John felt as though he was traveling back in time, so much was this place like The Saucy Maiden in Plymouth, across the sea in England.

They spent two weeks there, restocking their supplies of corn and balls and powder, all the things they would need, buying heavy knit caps, thick mittens, and warmer leggings for the three of them. The purse Lord MacNeil had slipped into John's hand the night before he left contained more than enough coins for their needs. The

days passed on, a calm island of paper and charcoal drawings. John wished to sketch, to draw this place and its
people for himself as well as for the King. How long
would it be until he returned? Their provisions replen-
ished and warm clothing on their backs, they set out
again, ready for the last leg of their journey.

As it was, the weather remained mild. John knew that
two years ago it would have seemed much harsher to
him. Some snow fell, but most days were sunny and only
light winds blew. John enjoyed traveling with his friends,
Wallace and Natka.

It was spring when they arrived in the port of New
York. John would sail soon. His companions planned a
leisurely return to Lake Erie. A week, perhaps, to make
preparations, then John would be gone and Wallace and
Natka would travel back to Fort Detroit. The *Amazon*
waited for him as his father had said, solid and steady and
utterly English. How amazing it was to see her tied there
at the wharf with the British flag waving on her staff.
Like a well-known ghost, a familiar form came striding
down the deck and a deep voice boomed out. He has not
changed at all, thought John, waving to the huge man.

"Ahoy, young John!" called Tom Apple. "I see you
survived the wilds of Canada!"

"Ahoy, Tom Apple! That I did!" answered John, as he
led Wallace and Natka up the gangplank. What tales
they all exchanged at the tavern where John and his
friends stayed that evening.

The night before the *Amazon* sailed, John had a dream.
In it, he saw Marie paddling her canoe into a pale, soft

fog. Her back was straight and she faced whatever it was that lay beyond her vision with bravery. At the last moment, just before the canoe's bow slipped into the pearly whiteness, she turned. She smiled, her eyes fixed warmly on his, and raised her hand in farewell. The dragonfly on her wrist made a small blue flash. Then she was gone, swallowed by the cloudy mist.

It was there on the dock the next afternoon, as they were saying their farewells, that the news reached John. The Miami runner who brought the letter nearly collapsed from exhaustion. He had raced through the forests for many days to find John MacNeil. John opened the lumpy, oiled packet.

"Are you well, lad? It canna be good news." Wallace scarcely needed to ask. He stared at the circle of silver John now held in his hand. The last time Wallace had seen it, Pierre had slipped the ring on Marie's finger the day they said their wedding vows.

John would never forget that awful shock of first reading the letter. A robin sang in the still spring air, and he could feel the growing warmth of the sun on the back of his neck and legs. Somewhere a dove called for its mate. It was a beautiful day.

*My dear John,* Pierre's letter began. *I can think of no other way to tell this. Marie is gone.*

John read the letter to its end. He could scarcely breathe. All the sounds of the harbor had been there a second ago. But now the voices of sailors calling to each other and the noise of merchants and travelers arguing and bargaining all disappeared. It was as though he was in a glass bubble of silence. There had to be a mistake. Surely if he just walked along the wharf in the sunshine, all would be well. He carefully folded the letter and with stiff fingers, placed it back in the packet. Then he turned his back on his friends and walked alone for a long while.

The Miami messenger gave the news to Wallace and Natka. Smallpox had taken so many. There were rumors that blankets infected with the disease had deliberately been given to the Natives. General Amherst had ordered it done, they said. LaButte should count himself lucky that he still had the son his wife had borne him. The troubles had begun and there was war on the lakes. How fortunate that Lord MacNeil had been sent out from Detroit a month before. He was not far behind them, having only a few days ago reached Albany with dispatches.

When John returned to the *Amazon* some hours later, he sat in Captain Blair's cabin and wrote a last letter to his sister. He would not leave for England on this ship, he had decided. He would wait for his father instead. The ship rocked gently under him as he dipped his quill into the ink again and again. Finally he sat back and blotting the paper, slipped it into an envelope. He melted and dripped sealing wax on the envelope's flap and pressed the hot lump with his stamp. As tired as though he had run many leagues, he rose and went onto the deck. Tom Apple stood there leaning against the rail. Natka and Wallace were with him, their eyes watchful and concerned.

"See that Jane gets this letter, Tom. It has important things in it for her."

"I shall bring it to her myself when we reach Plymouth," assured the seaman. How sad John looked. Was it so hard for him to be leaving this country? Ah, he would perk up again once he was back in England with civilized folk. He watched the boy's straight back as he left the ship with his companions.

"God speed then, John," shouted Captain Blair later, as the *Amazon* prepared to sail out on the evening tide. Another ship, the *Willow*, would take John and his father back to England in a few weeks. John held up his hand in farewell.

"God speed, sir," he called back. He stood on the wharf with Wallace and Natka as the graceful ship left for home. Home? thought John. Where is my home now? Not England, certainly. I do think it might be back somewhere upon a small island near the mouth of a fast-flowing river. He looked up as someone spoke.

"We will stay with you until your father arrives," said Natka, squeezing John's shoulder. Natka smiled sadly to himself as he watched John who looked so lost and alone.

"This shouldna have happened. Not war, not the deaths," growled Wallace. He shook his head. The poor lad. 'Twas a hard thing to know that a young friend had died. His heart went out even more to LaButte, who had lost his wife and now had a bairn to raise alone. Wallace knew how difficult that was, since his own sweet lass had passed on. He still felt the sting of his loss, even these many years later.

"Let us go back to the inn," said John quietly. Then he turned suddenly to the two men, his face lit with an idea. "Come with us. Come to England and to Brierly." Wallace and Natka exchanged looks as they considered the prospect.

At the inn they sat in the common room in front of the hearth and talked for hours as the fire burned low. It would be no small thing, this journey across the ocean so far from the things that were familiar to them.

"I havna seen that part of the world in a long while," mused Wallace finally, pulling off his bonnet and scratching his head. "It'll be safe enough on the lakes for anyone who is French, and so LaButte and the Roys will be well. I must send word to the wee lads, mind you now. It isna a good time to be leaving them on their own with war so near, but I ken they're old enough at last, and they'll be protected by the Miamis." He regarded Natka and their eyes met in sudden agreement. There was time enough for the lad to face the world on his own. For now he needed his two old friends with him for a little while longer.

"It will be interesting," said Natka with a serious face. There was a moment of silence and then the two men burst into laughter. Although he could not laugh, John smiled. How good even that felt.

◇ ◇

Weeks later, in the late summer, Lady Jane MacNeil sat in the morning room at Brierly. She held a small child on her lap. He wiggled a bit and reached for her spectacles, but Jane was quite accustomed to dodging the dear, little hands. She stroked Jamie's fair, curling hair and then read the letter again. Viscount Henry Fitzwalter peered owlishly over her shoulder and read John's letter with her.

*My dearest Jane, you must know that I will return home at the command of King George. With luck and clear sailing I shall see you at Brierly before the fall. Father will be with me. He left Fort Detroit not a month after I did. He has news for the Crown of the desperate situation in Canada.*

*I have so much to tell you, Jane, things both happy and so very sad. I believe I shall wait until we can again sit in my room as we once did. What a comfort it will be to share it all with you. And then there shall be your wedding! How fine that day will be.*

*I wish I could have brought back all of the people I came to know and cherish in Canada, but that is not possible, I fear. Perhaps some day you will meet them, and come to understand the reasons I so love this wilderness.*

*There is a small packet here for you. It was sent by Marie LaButte with the letter her husband penned for her. It is her wedding gift for you. She said to tell you that she wishes the two of you might have met. That can never be, Jane. She wants to give you a part of the place where I think in the end, we all were the happiest, a small part of that island she loved so well. She said to say that sometimes you need look no further than what is right in front of you to find happiness.*

Both she and Henry stared at the portrait of Marie that John had included with his letter. The calm green eyes looked back at them, and Jane had the sense of someone she almost knew, someone who gazed out across a distance that was far greater than that of any ocean. How strange to read in Marie's words the very thing she herself now understood. She no longer envied John's life and what he did. She believed she had found the path her own future would take, and each day was a grand adventure. Who could say what places she would see and what things she might do in years ahead?

Jane opened the packet. A handful of small seeds rested inside, brown teardrops against the white paper.

"They are apple seeds," laughed Henry in delight. "We shall take them to the potting shed and begin the seedlings at once. Let us plant our own orchard, Jane. A small one I think, where in time our own children might play." He gently turned the seeds with his finger. "I wonder what sort of fruit they will bear?"

"I expect the apples will be very sweet, indeed, my love," Jane said softly as she slipped off her spectacles. Then she stood, and with small Jamie in her arms, went to tell Lady Emma that John and Father were coming home.

## A U T H O R ' S
## N O T E S

History is a matter of interpreting what we know. The artifacts and primary documents that paint a picture of the past are essential tools. They are the proof of what was there and what occurred. In the writing of historical fiction, there is another key element: imagination. The idea of what might have happened, the glittering prospect of what if, has its own importance. Tucked within all the pages of history are the untold stories of people who might have moved in that dark dance of adventure.

John MacNeil is such a character. He and his family are fictional; they lived only in the pages of this book. However, many of the other characters in *A Circle of Silver* were real people. Pontiac did form an alliance of the tribes. He united them into a powerful force and the rebellion that resulted in the summer of 1763 very nearly succeeded. Forts up and down the lakes were taken; Fort Detroit was one of those that held fast. General Amherst, Captain Campbell, and Major Gladwin were all part of the struggle. Lieutenant Jeffery Lindsay, being a fictional character, was not. That is fortunate for him since, when

Fort Michilimackinac fell, almost every occupant was either taken prisoner or killed.

Death came in many forms in those days, and smallpox was a particular curse if you were unlucky enough to contract it. During Pontiac's Rebellion smallpox took on an even more sinister nature. There is clear evidence that General Amherst not only knew that infected blankets were being given to the tribes, his own papers show that he was in support of such a plan.

As for Pierre LaButte and Marie Roy, they were my grandparents eight generations back and it is through Pierre that my maternal family traces part of its history. Pierre was a man of influence, important for more than the fact that he was one of the translators between the British and Pontiac. He became a merchant and held several contracts to deliver goods between Montreal and Detroit. Although his home and apple trees were destroyed by the British during the siege of Fort Detroit, for the purposes stated by Gladwin in this story, Pierre continued to live in his home on Ste. Anne Street. When he died in 1774, he was buried beneath the altar of Ste. Anne's Church at Fort Detroit.

It is with regard to Pierre's and Marie's lives that I have taken liberty in this book. He would have been a middle-aged man during that summer. Marie Roy, whom he did marry in 1728, would already have been dead from smallpox when this story takes place. In giving Pierre back his youth and allowing Marie to live a little longer, I involved them in an adventure that they surely would have enjoyed.

---◇---

# ACKNOWLEGEMENTS

As with the creation of all stories, there was a small army of people moving about in the background as I wrote *A Circle of Silver*. In this case it was Les Compagnies du Détroit, the Detroit Marines, the living history unit of which I am a member. It is the original Marines who manned Fort Detroit during the French period. The members of Les Compagnies du Détroit are a continual source of inspiration; all those conversations via email and by candlelight were truly helpful.

I am most grateful to Andy Gallup, who read the manuscript, fine-tuned historical facts of the period, and with his knowledge of the period, showed me the beginnings of how to think in eighteenth century terms; to Donald Shaffer who answered endless inquiries with patience and good humor, providing me with details I could unearth nowhere else; and to George Bray, who kindly enlightened me on many small points regarding the British military of the time. To Clabert Menard who crafted the beautiful wampum belt and to Al Van Mil who painted the unique cover art and enlightened me regarding eighteenth-century drawing materials, my appreciation.

I especially thank Kathryn Cole and everyone at Stoddart Kids who had the vision to look back in time and see a future for this project. To Lynne Missen, my editor, who answered perhaps the oddest questions of all and who gave me direction, my gratitude.

But perhaps my greatest debt must go to Pierre LaButte and Marie Roy, the people whose lives made this book happen. Scholars and authors may take up their pens to record history, but it is really written by those who live the events. Through this story may their adventure live on.